Sandy Austrin-Miner was
graduated and worked in r
overland to Scotland wh
presently lives outside of E   mother to
her four children, writing as family demands permit.

Sandy Austrin-Miner

His Name is Love

Latent Publishing

Copyright © 2004 Sandy Austrin-Miner

First Published 2004 by Latent Publishing

06 05 04 03 02 01 00   7 6 5 4 3 2 1

Latent Publishing is an imprint of Latent Publishing Ltd.

Latent Publishing Ltd
PO Box 23919, Pathhead
SCOTLAND, EH37 5YG

www.latentpublishing.com

British Library Cataloguing in Publication Data

A catalogue record for this book is available from the
British Library.

ISBN 0-9548821-0-5

Printed and Bound in Scotland.

I.

She lies coiled like a tight shell, small and fragile in the hard bed. Stainless steel bars frame her tiny form, starched sheets tucked crisply around her. She hugs a bear, pressing her face into his woolly back, and sobs quietly.

Through her closed eyes she can see the frightened faces of her parents, eyes red and watery, mouths stretched into shallow smiles, voices trembling and thin. With a wavering hand, her mother strokes back her hair; an icy touch as it brushes against her cheek.

There is no warmth in the bed, no softness to huddle into. She shivers. Antiseptic clings to the still air and stings her nostrils. A light burns overhead, unrelenting; obscuring day and night. Footsteps beat to and fro; clatter and thud back and forth along the corridor outside. Trolleys clang their halting approach.

Low voices murmur in the shadow of her doorway. She strains to comprehend the mumbled tones. Words dart out in chilling clarity; "...not happy... unsuccessful...watch carefully..." She shrinks away from the glaring light and the careful voices, slides into the comforting darkness of her mind, and drifts along with the warmth and ease. Sounds fade away to a tumbling hum, a strand that stretches thinner and thinner, until there is just sweet, long darkness.

Suddenly, the darkness is interrupted by a light. It is not a harsh hospital light that blinks and stares, but a gentle light that glows softly around her, that dances and shimmers like early morning sunshine. She stretches in the comforting glow and searches the azure sky that domes her. Her eyes roam hesitantly, squinting in anticipation of the first stinging shafts of light from the fiery ball. The sky is clear and stretches in a flawless arc of blue. She sits up, puzzled. "Where is the sun?"

She sees that she is in a garden. She blinks several times and rubs her eyes. The colours are more vivid than she can ever remember and seem to sparkle like jewels. She turns slowly around, her breath caught in her small beating chest. She is standing on a spreading lawn that dips and rolls gracefully in a gentle slope that reaches across to the curving shores of a small lake. The garden is arrayed with flowers and shrubs, dotted with clusters of arching trees, sprinkled with flowers. Her eyes sweep back and forth across the view in wonder. She stoops to run her pale fingers across the grass. "Like velvet" she whispers. She draws in the sweet scent of the warm grass, tinged with the perfume of flowers; it's the smell of a perfect summer's day, full of laughter and blue skies.

She steps carefully across the lawn and meanders between the beds of flowers with upturned faces, masses of blooms bursting with colour. Great columns of trees stand in dignified groups, lifting their elegant boughs, hung with ripe fruit of every kind. She sways, her head reeling with perfume and colours and the warm air.

From across the lawn she is sure she can hear the sound of water trickling; a musical fountain of water flowing nearby. But above that sound she can hear something else; a sound like voices drifting in songs; soft tunes wafting through the trees. Lulled by the gentle chorus, she winds serenely through the garden.

A rustling noise behind startles her and she swings around. Her eyes widen and her breath freezes as the long, sand-coloured body of a lion moves stealthily, quietly from among the bushes, and pads nobly across the grass towards her. A second beats slowly past as she waits for fear to explode in crashing waves through her weak body, and for the lion to leap snarling, clawing, ripping, onto her. She waits, held strangely calm by the singing voices that float around her. She stands watching. His great body curves silently around her, brushing softly against her legs, and lumbers away across the grass. Her astonished eyes are still following him, when a flurry behind her grabs her attention. A small lamb bursts bleating from the same bush and skips off behind the lion, nudging him playfully. Dazed, she finds herself following them, moving deeper into the garden. And then she can see that the garden is teeming with all kinds of creatures; the strong protecting the weak, the great comforting the small, the hunter lying with the prey.

The dancing stream catches her ears again and she follows the sound as it beckons and calls, through the garden, around the shores of the lake, to the base of a tree. Baffled, she stops at the gnarled tree; the bubbling and gurgling of water seems to be coming from within its broad trunk. She looks up into its branches, twisted and knotted with great age, surprised to see that it is bursting with fruit. Gazing into its lofty boughs, she circles the tree until she discovers the stream, emptying into its base; water seeping invisibly away.

She turns and follows the stream as it leads her through a leafy copse out into open space again. She eyes the grassy slope ahead, the stream disappearing over the brow of a hill and dipping out of sight. She feels weak and breathless at just the thought of climbing such a slope. The ringing voices grow louder, sailing down the hill, circling her spinning head, drawing her upwards. Her feet begin to step lightly over the grass, carrying her forward and up. Her chest expands easily, drawing in deep breathfulls of warm, clean air. Her eyes are fixed ahead on the crest of the hill. The fuzziness in her head begins to melt away bringing her surroundings into sharper distinction, like a woolly veil being drawn away to reveal something fresh and new. Her feet seem to be growing lighter and lighter, weight floating away, effort dissipating. An airy spring creeps into her step as she strides along, her body waxing with new vigour and broadening with strength. Her gait begins to stretch and bound, and she finds to her surprise that she is running effortlessly up the hill, shaking-off all her sickness and weariness, and finding herself infused with vitality.

A dark form swoops out of the endless sky, and glides above her. As it circles and spirals down on its broad wing span, she sees it is an eagle sailing towards her. It dips over her, beating the air with its powerful wings. A rush of air smacks against her face. The bird turns and soars away, climbing the mountain before her in one graceful breath. Her face glows with a joyful smile and her laughter rings into the clear air. Lightness overcomes her striding body and she is carried in one soaring movement like the eagle's flight, rushing up the steep climb of the mountain, till she is standing breathless and dazed at the shimmering apex, looking dizzily around her.

She turns slowly to catch all the land around her in her hungry gaze; the rolling hills tumbling away; the stream trickling down like a ribbon of sparkling silver threads; the lake still, like a deep sapphire, light glinting across its glassy surface. She stands trembling at the top, the view filling her eyes and heart; feeling almost overwhelmed by the intensity of the beauty, like she must faint or cry or laugh. Her eyes move slowly over each perfect detail until they alight on something so wondrous that she is stopped instantly. She stares, caught in unblinking silence, reeling with the splendour, her breath stilled, her heart thrumming palpably. Rising majestically out of the rocky peak of the highest mountain is a palace so magnificent that all the beauty around it grows pale. Built of pure gold, its walls shine like the burning midday sun, spreading light through the land; illuminating the sky. Its windows glitter like precious jewels, its towers disappearing into the arching blue sky.

She looks down. The winding stream is like a path at her feet, curving across the mountain ridge, leading her to its source. She follows it with timid steps as it leads her closer and closer to the great palace. The singing grows louder as she is drawn nearer. The air resonates with chiming voices as they ring and toll out from the golden walls and across the mountaintops. The stream broadens and gurgles as it runs, chattering excitedly. A warm sense of longing spreads through her; anticipation buzzing eagerly.

The palace grows enormous overhead as she reaches the rocky base of its towering buttresses. The palace is encircled by a great wall, but as she follows the stream, now a rushing river, she is lead to a massive gate. She gasps to discover that the gate is carved entirely from shimmering pearl and is swung open in an extravagant gesture of welcome. Looking tentatively around, she walks in.

The river courses ahead, so she follows it still as it runs through an ornate garden and up to the palace doors. The doors are huge, studded with richly coloured jewels, and they too are thrown wide open. Her burning curiosity overwhelms her timidity; she climbs the few steps and enters in through the great portal. She moves forward anticipating gloomy shadows as she steps away from the clear light outside. Instead, she is startled to find herself bathed in light even more brilliant and luminous. She looks around, squinting, adjusting to the radiance.

She finds she is in a massive hall, rows of columns stretching like a great avenue, the domed ceiling floating high above like a canopy. Down the centre of the room extends a long table set for a magnificent feast. She runs her eyes along the length of table, set with gleaming gold dishes for hundreds and hundreds of places, mounded high with rich and exotic food. She scans the great stretching room, surprised to find it empty apart from herself, the food an untouched and waiting display of extravagance.

Everything is still except for the stream of dancing water cutting across the banquet hall and disappearing through a great arching doorway at the far side of the hall. Light blazes out of the opening in dazzling whiteness, choruses ringing through the screen of brightness. Dazed, she steps haltingly up to the doorway, finding the shimmering light irresistible, enchanted by the singing stream. She peers blindly through the brightness, seconds flickering by as she strains to see what has already seen her.

She catches the glint and rush of the water, and her eyes bring her new surroundings into focus. She sways as faintness floods over her, almost sweeping her to the ground. She staggers under powerful torrents of emotion; something like fear: shrinking, melting, curling up; something like happiness: expanding, exploding, warm and clear.

The river springs from the foot of a great, golden throne, which stands in the centre of a shimmering sea of crystal, and is circled by a rainbow that flashes like an emerald. Seated on the throne is the source of the light and the stream. Through the airy light she sees the form of a man. He is dressed in gleaming white with the splendour and radiance of jewels, sashed with gold. His whole appearance glows, with snow-white hair and eyes like burning fire. His voice rushes out with the musical flow of the stream. She gazes at his face. It is shining with all the brilliance of the midday sun, radiating light through the palace and all the hills and gardens that she had passed through, yet is infused with all the kindness and gentleness that she has ever encountered. In a rocking, nauseous moment she feels herself smack heavily against the cold, hard floor.

His voice washes over her in a velvet whisper, "Do not be afraid."

She opens her eyes. She is hovering amidst a multitude of people robed in glistening white, crowding around the throne. Their joyful voices swell as one resounding note that rings in praise of their King with loud "Hallelujahs". Her own voice surges out to join the exultant chord. She hears echoing in her own heart and singing on her lips, the tune that had whispered and hummed in her ears through the enchanted garden.

The singing suddenly stops, and everyone is poised in expectant silence.

The King is mounted on His throne, surrounded by all He has made; His servants encircling Him in bowing reverence, performing His will as his word directs. They stream in and out of His presence with reports of what has been achieved and done. One sits at the King's feet. He is the most beautiful and powerful creature ever spoken into existence. He smiles and stretches in the warmth of the King's praise; a star shining bright amidst a dazzling constellation.

A trumpet voice thunders out from the throne and percusses gently through the host, resonating the fringes of eternity; pregnating reality with His imagination. Immediately, the servant leaps up from His feet and glides away through the main doors. The rest wait, still in the lingering chord of His command, watching steadily. After a time the servant returns, his face lit with delight.

"Lord, it is all done exactly as you said; everything is according to your word. There, in the place of the desolate plain, is a beautiful city, watered and planted with all kinds of living things, inhabited by families of good people, and teeming with creatures."

Then a sound like the roar of a wave or a peal of thunder spreads through the immense crowd, the sound of thousands and tens of thousands of voices praising and shouting, "Hallelujah".

"Well, my good Servant, you shall be governor of the town. You shall rule it according to my way and teach all the people my laws, so they can work and live in peace and love. And you will tell them all about me, their King, and how they were created out of love, for love."

The Servant bows and slides gracefully away, face effused with joy and love. A purr of pleasure circles through the multitude, and quietly grows into a clear note that resonates louder and louder, till it dances and floats with ringing tunes that echo through infinity.

His Name is Love

II.

The King's Servant circled in the sky like a drifting breeze. The city below appeared miniature in gleaming white marble, crawling with the scurry and bustle of activity. It magnified to grander proportions as he swooped gracefully down, settling on the strong walls that surround the burgh.

"I have done what He commanded," reflected the servant pensively. "I have given them laws to live by and they do live peaceful and productive lives; I have given them His love and they have flourished in it, blossoming in love and creativity." His eyes roamed over the spread of homes and gardens, and criss-cross of streets, with a vague sense of frustration and sad longing.

"And they do love Him. They have never seen Him, yet they love Him as their own father." The servant exhaled with a long, slow breath; but the dull, sick pain remained lodged in his chest. "They love Him because of what I have said and done." Envy flickered through his heart like a struck match.

The servant moved invisibly through the ebbing stream of townsfolk, gliding silently towards the market square. The cobbled square was still quite empty, it's sunny planes streaked with long morning shadows, cloistered by the rows of tall buildings that flanked the square on four sides. Shop fronts peered out through arches of ornately carved stone, their windows gleaming with prosperity; strung like a row of jewels. The servant hurried through the arcade without noticing the shops or offices, his thoughts set on the morning's event. He swept past the lavish facades of towering buildings, storeys of grandeur layered like a wedding cake, stopping only when he reached the most splendid and imposing of all. The Town Hall was an immense building of palatial proportions, embellished with colonnades and scrolls, trailed with gilt. The servant slunk surreptitiously into the shadowy entrance of the portico and disappeared into its recesses. From there he watched over the square.

In the centre of the square, obscured by a drape that hung over it, was a tall object that stood erect like a pillar. Beyond it a platform was being constructed. The servant watched as chairs were carried up and spaced uniformly along its breadth, and garlands of flowers were trailed and hung over its surface. The morning hummed by, the shadows shrinking back to the edges of the square and slowly revolving like a great sundial. As the long hands of the town hall clock crept towards Eleven, people started to gather around the platform in a gaily dressed crowd that gently stirred with excitement. The sun beamed down on shiny ribbons and laughing faces as more and more festive people squeezed into the square.

With the striking of the hour, a hush spread in waves over the sea of bobbing faces. A small procession crawled ant-like out of the shadows of the town hall portico and filed solemnly across the sunlit cobbles. The mute crowd watched the cortege of statesmen climb onto the stage and formally assemble themselves on the chairs. Trailing languidly behind was the Servant. He mounted the stairs and sauntered casually behind the row of dignitaries. The Mayor stood up and shuffled towards the front of the stage to welcome the crowd and begin the proceedings. The Servant strolled over to the Mayor's side and leant towards his ear. "I'm here," he whispered. The Mayor, his eyes still addressing the crowd, smiled with a sense of confidence, and mouthed in reply, "Governor."

While the Mayor spoke in praise of their King who had created them and blessed them with wealth and peace, teaching them all good things, the crowd looked on attentatively, nodding and smiling in approbation. The Servant jumped down from the stage and pushed his way through the crowd. He thrust his face up close to those enraptured faces, examining their countenances, sighing in their ears. But he remained invisible and unheard.

The speeches ended and everyone turned to watch the unveiling. With a pull of a chord the drape slid noiselessly to the ground revealing the tribute beneath. A sculpted crown sat elevated on a high plinth, and below it the words inscribed, "In Our King We Trust." The people cheered and wept, their love spilling out in songs and dancing. The town leaders smiled happily to each other.

A small boy's voice piped softly but persistently, "Daddy, Daddy, I can't see." Strong arms reached down to him and in a single sweeping motion, hoisted him onto his father's shoulders. Pleasure radiated from the boy's eyes as he looked over the dancing crowd. His gaze rested on the statue.

"But what does it mean?"

His father's voice called up from the jostle and noise. "The crown represents our king. It stands there to remind us of His love for us."

The boy stared intently at the monument, mouthing silently the words of the inscription. He looked around at the crowd again, and something of their love and trust crept into his heart, warming him, like the sun when it steals in through a window on a wintry day, its light touching the ordinary, gilding it with beauty. In a shuddering, expanding moment, the King materialized as a real person out of the cartoon reality of his bedtime stories. His mind thrilled with sudden clarity as the King's presence exploded in his consciousness.

"Now I believe."

The Servant stared at the monument, then gazed blankly at the rejoicing crowd. That small flame of envy that had been smouldering all morning, suddenly ignited a raging fire that raced and burned through his whole magnificent being, scorching and devastating his soul and intentions. His beautiful face twisted and contorted with an agonizing scream. Hate spread in a destroying wave, ravaging his mind, leaving his heart blackened and cold. He looked perniciously at the people and hissed savagely, "I will make you serve me."

The servant stole malevolently back through the crowd towards the stage. He stared at the Mayor who was smiling and swaying with the dancing tunes, beating the air with his arms as if he was conducting the whole crowd. The servant's lips curled scornfully as he sidled up to the Mayor and breathed noxiously into his thoughts. "Shouldn't this be you they are all worshipping, it's you who does all the work for them, not Him. He doesn't even show his face here. Just picture yourself on that pedestal gazing nobly down on the square." The Servant slipped silently away leaving his words to spread venomously through the man's mind, poisoning his heart, pricking his pride.

For a moment the Mayor's beating arms faltered and froze mid-air. Scarlet heat rushed through his cheeks and a strange sense of discontent stirred deep within him. He shook away his menacing thoughts and took up the tempo again with his arms.

The following day the square was empty except for a roving, pecking flock of pigeons, alighting and settling again in a petulant wave. The Mayor stepped blinking into the midday sun, his shoes striking a confident click across the cobble-stones. His stride swelled with satisfaction as he eyed the town centre. He reflected happily on his own contribution and, as he strolled along through the sunny streets, the greatness of his achievement became clearer to him.

"I'm not a proud man," he thought to himself. "It's always been my joy just to serve other people. But I do wonder what would have happened to this place if I had not been here to organize everything."

A shadowy figure skulked noiselessly beside him, lurking in the shady overhang of the buildings, slipping invisibly from one doorway to the next.

A honey voice dripped seductively into his thoughts. "But does anyone realise? Does anyone appreciate what you have done?" The Servant slid back into the pool of shadows.

"No! They think it is the King who has done all this. Alright, he may have started things off in the beginning, but it's been men like me who have devoted themselves to leading the people, and working for peace and prosperity, that have made the town what it is."

The Mayor's cheeks burned and his chest tightened with indignation as he strode briskly along the wide streets, bristling with annoyance. He raised a sweaty hand to shield himself from the glaring rays of sun. The paved streets turned into leafy avenues and lead him in a great arc until he re-entered the square at the opposite side. He stepped heavily into the centre and stood at the base of the statue, squinting up at the crown; a golden ring gleaming in the cloudless heavens.

He saw himself, carved in smooth, white marble, smiling down from a clear, blue sky; the blazing sun crowning him. His brittle wall of anger softened and melted away. Heat stole through his veins as his blood beat hot, stirring him deeply. Brief snatches of honour flashed through his heart and cinematographic images played in his mind. He walked distractedly back to the town hall, his face beaming with colour.

The Servant leant against the plinth and watched him leave, smiling knowingly.

III.

Smoke swirls ominously around the King's throne. Thunder rumbles over the frightened hush, and strikes with lightening flares. A tempest simmers overhead. The King is slumped low in dejection. Pain streaks His face and wracks His soul. Everyone is waiting.

A dark figure worms his way into view, shrinking in the intense light, cowering from the King's face. The multitude murmur in shocked whispers. He waits, wretched in his own condemnation.

"I sent you in my name, with my love, to serve them, not to pervert them. You have turned against me and cut yourself off. You are no longer mine. You can never return here." The King's words fall like heavy stones dashing against His pain.

The multitude brim with expectation. "He'll remember his love, he'll show that he's sorry and plead for mercy." They are sure. They remember the shining one, full of strength and beauty.

Darkness condenses in his soul and brews contempt. He sneers scornfully. "I have my own kingdom now. I don't need to be subject to you."

The King's whisper echoes powerfully, "For a time. So it seems. But just for a time."

His Name is Love

IV

Steam rose in swirling clouds from pans that clattered and clanged on the stove as dinner bubbled and boiled. Joseph lent back in the wooden chair that perched under the window and watched his mother as she moved lightly around the kitchen. His eyes unconsciously followed her as he sat with his head tilted dreamily, his arms wrapped around his folded legs. His kicking, schoolboy energy had all seeped away as he sank into the languor that accompanied this special part of the day. A quiet stillness filled him as he was lulled by the gentle, familiar sounds of tea-time; the clink of china as plates were set, the tinkling pan lids, mother's soft voice trailing wisps of song, the bits she could remember. He turned his gaze to the window, and watched a mob of pigeons circle in a dark crescent against the thin wash of sky.

High pitched voices called to the children still playing in the street, children shrieking over the rhythmic patter of their games, a ball echoing a deep thud, thud, thud. A car engine drew to a humming halt. Joseph watched the dark suited man squeeze himself out of the car, and push through the laughing, clamouring crowd of his children as they chimed excitedly with things they had to tell him, clung to his legs as he tried to walk, climbed on his back and begged to be carried. The corners of his lips were tucked into a deep smile as he lumbered towards his front door. Mother's soft eyes met her son's.

"Your father's home."

The closing of the front door rang through the house and the laughing, giggling uproar edged its way up the hall. Joseph waited in that last, still second as twilight curtained the window throwing a transparent, uncertain light across the kitchen, savouring the stillness that was pregnant with his quiet thoughts, anticipating that sudden burst of noise. Mother kept working; her back turned to the door, she still kept up the patter of her work. Even as the whooping, cheering mass of her family reeled into the kitchen, her hands moved quickly and skilfully, her long neck curved away from their entrance. Father shook one hand free and gently placed it on her shoulder, drawing it towards him. In one moment, a moment Joseph loved, she put down her busy knife and turned to him and her bubbling brood of children. And as she turned, Joseph watched to catch her face. He lent forward to catch that lovely moment which seemed to typify his childhood happiness, when her face turned, and full of shining joy, met his father. Her dark eyes were deep, moist pools, her lips parted in a smile. Father leant across the mass of bobbing heads to kiss her smooth cheek and a tint of rose crept through her ivory skin.

Shaking children loose, father strode across the kitchen to Joseph's window perch. His hand smoothed the boy's hair and slid down the side of his face till it rested on his shoulder. "How's my biggest boy?"

"Fine," Joseph grinned in reply.

"Then come and help me get everyone to the table. Right; I want hands washed and children on chairs." His singing voice resonated around the kitchen as a scurry of giggling children raced around the table and disappeared down the hall, fleeing his instructions. He beckoned Joseph with a tilt of his head and a look of cheerful resignation. Together they stomped and whooped after the shrieking little ones as mother ladled food onto plates, her face lit with fond amusement. They did this every night. His good humoured lumbering games and her quiet shining eyes never gave a clue to the fear and tension they lived with.

Father eyed the children that circled the table, faces still trembling with stifled giggles. "O.K. We've had our fun. It's time to be serious now as we remember who always makes sure we have enough. Let's give thanks for our food. 'Our Lord and King, we thank you for your love and faithfulness, for your goodness in all that you've given us, and for this food now.'"

A clatter of cutlery resounded as the children hungrily began their meal. Mother and father paused to share a smile before beginning to eat. Joseph watched them all thoughtfully.

"Dad," a small voice piped. "Why do we have to give thanks for our meal when everyone says that the King doesn't really exist?"

Mother's eyes dropped sadly to the table, her lashes brushing softly on her cheeks. Father coughed slightly and placed his knife carefully on his plate.

"What do people say, Ben?"

Ben's face coloured as everyone stopped eating to listen. "Well, that there isn't really any King, it's just a story people told each other a long time ago."

"And what do you think?" came his steady reply.

"I don't know." stammered Ben uncertainly.

"It's time to know; for all of you to know what you believe. Each one of you will have to live by what you believe, and answer for how you have lived." He paused as they all stared uncomfortably at him and his sober words hung heavily over the table. "Ah. You're all so young." His voice trailed away painfully. Silence spread over the waiting meal. "If He is just a story then nothing makes sense;" he muttered, "we don't make sense."

Father and Joseph strolled through the empty streets as the sky deepened in inky hues, and street lamps burst into yellow pools of light. Their steps echoed softly between the houses that murmured with the evening sounds; the muffled voices of younger children resisting sleep, a mother's call ringing impatiently for silence, doors closing against the cool of night, occasional cars humming distantly.

"Father, what did you mean at tea-time?" Joseph broke the silence they had fallen into.

"Hmm," Father replied dreamily as his long legs swung beside Joseph's thoughtful frame.

"That we don't make sense, if He doesn't exist. What difference does it make?"

Father's forehead wrinkled as he wrestled with the question. "The difference is whether we were made intentionally for a purpose or whether we are just the result of an accident, a random event. Whether we were made by an all powerful creator because he wanted us to exist; so that we can enjoy him and his love, and have the opportunity to love him and each other for ever; or whether we are the result of a series of random chemical reactions and nothing has any more significance than how it makes us feel. What if I can't feel good any more? What if I'm poor and can't have the things I want? What if I'm sick or disabled and don't have the power to make my life worthwhile? What is the purpose of having a life if the means of enjoying it or being successful in it can be lost so easily? The reality is that we want our lives to mean something, we cannot reconcile ourselves to the thought that our lives have no significance. But if I'm made by someone to be loved, and His character makes that love an unbreakable certainty, all that I need do is respond and my life is fulfilled. Anything outside of that, that I find or lose, achieve or fail, are just small finds and achievements, losses and failures, pleasures or disappointments; and while they may be wonderful or painful, they do not constitute me or my life; my reason for being." Father paused and looked down into Joseph's small boyish face, still frowning with the weight of his considerations.

"Does that all sound a bit too complicated?" Father's voice emptied sadly into the streets.

Joseph continued on in silence, his strides lengthening to meet his father's, but coming a little short so that every little while he had to make a little skip to catch up.

Joseph's voice rose in clear, flute-like tones, "It's a little hard to understand it all now but I will think about it."

The moon was shedding a silvery stream of light across the market square as they stepped out of the street and into the open space. Joseph watched the smooth face of his father contort with emotion as he laboured with his thoughts.

"I wish I could give you understanding but you will have to struggle with it for yourself."

"That's O.K. Dad. I can do that."

A long shadow cut like a dark slash across the brightly lit square. Joseph's eyes travelled along the shadow to where it met the base of a tall column. He followed the dark stem-like column as it rose high above the ground, meeting eventually the darkened face of a man who towered over the square, his marble eyes staring blindly over the affairs of the town beneath.

"I was younger than you when I watched them unveil the original statue; a gleaming crown that symbolised our faith in the King. I sat on my father's shoulders and looked over the crowd that seemed to swell and ripple with some common emotion that I was an outsider to. I didn't know how to believe, but somehow as I was watching something beautiful crept into my heart."

"And then you just believed?" Joseph's small voice continued.

"Well, sort of. I had a feeling of Him and of His love; a strong, wonderful feeling that I thought would last for ever and would carry me through life. But of course it didn't."

"It didn't?" Joseph's voice was tinged with disappointment.

"No. But it was a start. It opened my heart to start learning about Him, to see how He helped me day by day. Little by little my trust grew until the reality of Him seemed as sure and certain as stone, a gold thread woven through the ordinary things of life making them all beautiful. Your understanding and faith need to be strong or they won't withstand the onslaught of these times." Father stared up at the immobile face of the statue, his face creased with pain. "The times are getting harder and harder for those of us who believe."

Joseph felt fear creeping through him like a cold shadow as he watched the seriousness of his father's face.

"So, what happened to the old statue, the one you saw unveiled?" Joseph's question broke into his father's silence.

Father's voice continued on in a thin, strained note. "It was smashed to the ground one night. According to the newspaper, by a marauding band of hoodlums. It always surprised me how quickly the new statue went up. How easily the plans were approved, how quiet the objections. How far we'd come from being a community that honoured the King to one that wanted to follow a man whose conceit was so great that..." Father's voice fell away as he looked up into the stone, unseeing eyes of the statue.

"What happened to him?" Joseph's voice was pushing, insisting.

"He gorged himself on public money, became more concerned with his own success than his civic duties, he and a few others grew fat until the ordinary people felt the pinch of it and became discontented. They'd loosed themselves from the King, but instead of going back when things started collapsing, they roamed around for a new leader with a new way that was going to succeed; going to give them everything they wanted."

Joseph followed pensively as his father turned and began their walk home.

"So, there you have it. A society governed by everyone's individual pursuit of what they want, and a succession of leaders who gain popularity by promising to fulfil dreams and lose it when they fail to please everyone. Chaos." Father's voice deepened. "There are not many of us who hold onto the Truth. Feelings have raged against the King so much that it is becoming dangerous to speak about him. On the one hand, He doesn't exist, so anyone can believe what they like and behave as they like, but on the other hand, all this mess and confusion is His fault. A community violently opposed to the memory of a being that never existed!"

The empty streets stretched silently ahead of them; their footsteps beat a sharp, syncopated tempo.

"And what about the people who say that the King is going to come one day?" Joseph's thoughts spilled into the dark night air.

"That is what is prophesied. A time will come when He will come down from His palace and will be among us."

"Aha!" rang Joseph's voice victoriously. "Then everyone will see. They'll see the King in real life and everyone will have to admit that it's Him."

"I wish it was that easy. The trouble is He won't necessarily appear as a king, or the way we think a king should be. It will be plain enough to those who love Him and are waiting for Him, but anyone who's heart is turned against Him won't see because they don't want to see."

"Well, how shall I know?" Joseph's small voice was piqued with exasperation at this circular reasoning.

"It has been passed on from generation to generation that He will reveal something that only a king could possibly have. It is this that we have to look for and recognise."

"And what if I miss it?" frustration was growing in Joseph's voice. "It's like a ridiculous game."

"If you're really looking with all your heart you won't miss it. Remember, He wants you to recognise Him; He wants you to be with Him. When He comes, it is to save us from this," Father's arms made a wide sweep of the street in emphasis, "not to play some mind game with us, that no-one can win." Father's voice lowered into a softer tone. "Don't be afraid. "If you want to know Him, He will reveal Himself to you."

They walked on in silence, with a quiet sense of closeness between them, their footsteps tapping into the empty streets.

A shout of laughter shattered the peace that had filled Joseph's dreamy thoughts. A raucous ring of hooting and shouting followed it. Joseph eyed the deserted street. A crowd of voices, ugly and menacing, reached them as a distant rumble, pierced with the sound of smashing glass and young screams. Joseph looked up to his father's face with fear and apprehension. Father carried the same calm, determined expression.

"It's alright, Joseph. They're a long way off. Don't be frightened."

The streets suddenly felt darker and the rows of houses stretched as faceless shadows. Father grasped Joseph's hand and continued his brisk step. The sound of small explosions cracked the night air, leaping out of the growing din of hoots and cries. Laughter cackled in sinister tones as the sound of wailing grew louder. Joseph had heard these sounds before as he had huddled in the warm safety of his bed, listening to the even breaths of his sleeping brothers as they sighed and turned in their dreams. Out here he felt vulnerable. The familiar streets around his house felt alien and unfriendly. Father's pace increased, his hard soled shoes snapping hurriedly along the road.

A low rumble, broken by loud cracking sounds, met their ears as they turned into their street. Father suddenly stopped; his eyes darted ahead, scanning the street. Footsteps retreated in a stumbling, disorderly mob as the sound of laughter floated away. Towards the end of the street the sky glowed with a strange orange light and the rumble grew louder, bursting with the sound of creaking timber.

Father dropped Joseph's hand and began to run. Terrified and confused, Joseph pursued him, his legs pounding the hard road. Breathless, Joseph raced along the road, struggling to keep up with his father, who was running faster than he'd ever run before. A deep wail broke from Father's throat as he drove his legs faster and faster along the street. Joseph fell further and further behind. Joseph watched the silhouetted form of his father collapse onto his knees; his hands clutching his head; his body writhing with agony. The road shortened as Joseph pounded towards the tormented figure of his father, panic screaming in his heart. He ran hard until he stood breathless and gasping beside his father's folded figure.

Sickness swept through Joseph in a crashing moment of realization: flames were tearing through his house and leaping up into the night sky.

Father turned his face, bloodless and streaked with tears, towards Joseph. Joseph trembled as his father heaved himself up onto his feet and lurched towards him. He reeled like a drunk man as he reached for Joseph, grabbing him roughly and pulling him near. Father squeezed Joseph with a savage intensity, crushing his small form against his heaving chest. His broken voice strained over the roar of flames that were engulfing the night. " I love you. Don't forget about Him." Bewildered, Joseph reached his arms around his father's waist hugging him, feeling the dampness of his sweat, tasting the tears that streamed down his face.

Father's strong hands clamped around Joseph's shoulders and he wrenched the boy's clinging body away from his. Joseph stared at his father's broken face as red light leapt and flickered across his pained expression, and heat flared in his cheeks. In a giddy, nauseous moment Joseph watched him turn and run; a dark form sprinting into the billowing, consuming flames. His anguished voice trailed behind him. "I must try to save them!"

Joseph's voice broke out of his screaming heart in a desperate, pursuing "No-o-o. No, Dad, No." He screamed hoarse and desperate into the roaring fire. His voice cried out mute and unheard into the empty street. Sobs wracked his crumpled body as he sank onto the cold, hard road.

He stayed there all night, huddled on the road, as the flames consumed his house; watching for the return of his father, waiting for someone from his family to emerge from the smoke and destruction. His neighbours' doors and windows stayed closed and silent. The bright flames filled the night then sank away to a dull glow which flickered and slowly ebbed away. Joseph crouched immobile in front of the charred, smoking ruin of his home as the ebony sky slowly faded into the dawn.

Rigid and dazed, Joseph stared at the blackened, steaming tangle of broken timbers and crumbled walls. His body ached with cold and fatigue. He caught the soft sounds of early morning breaking through the numbness of his grief; the chattering chorus of birds, the distant tread of footsteps, the scraping of doors. He felt suddenly exposed, crouching alone in the street; the street lined with houses closed and shuttered against him. Slowly he straightened his stiff legs and stood up, wavering unsteadily, disconnected from the street that stretched distantly around him. His senses were plunged in a heavy grey fog that chilled his reeling mind. Awkwardly, he stepped forward, sharp jolts of pain shooting up his legs as he moved them.

"Where do I go now?"

Absently he walked towards his smouldering home. Stepping over smoking piles of rubble he walked through the front doorway, feeling the still intense heat burn against his soles and face. As the thin sunlight broke through the dusky mauve of morning, he could recall the gentle sounds and smells of mother preparing breakfast. He could see the table laid with linen napkins and tumblers of juice, mother sipping tea as she made toast. The sick ball of pain squeezing his throat broke into hot, rolling streams of tears that tumbled down his face.

"Help me," he cried. "Someone please help me." His body shook with sobbing as he stood alone in the desolate ashes of his home and family.

V

"Enough!" His voice breaks like a weeping sigh into the lilting tunes that weave around His throne. "It has gone far enough, now is the time." The voices pause on a suspended note that hangs and shimmers beautifully around Him. Grief shadows His countenance. "Now all things must be made right." Expectation spreads like a rippling murmur through the multitude.

The King raises Himself wearily from His throne and slowly lifts His crown from His head, placing it carefully on the throne. Astonished eyes hover around Him; the cascading tune is lost in a gasp of dismay. He looks around at the circle of startled faces, feeling their alarm. "You always knew that this time would come, that I would have to complete what I began. Don't be afraid. I am still with you."

Silence permeates through the palace and the garden as all is stilled except the slow and deliberate motion of the King as He removes His garments of burning light; His robes of flashing gold slipping from His shoulders and lying in a shimmering pool at His feet. He gathers them together, draping them over His throne, and dresses Himself in the clothes of a man. Confused and bewildered, all shrink away from the diminished figure of a man they see standing in the place of the King.

His Name is Love

VI.

A sharp pang of fear passed through Joseph as he was startled out of his daze by a sudden noise nearby. Exhausted, he had passed from crying to staring absently with a strange sense of detachment, letting the images of the flames and his father tumble through his mind. A snapping noise suddenly broke the silence and he looked up. Peering through the broken fragments of wall he could see a stranger; a dark haired man in his thirties, standing on the far side of the house, in the garden, beckoning to him. Alarmed, he looked around and behind him. "Does he want me?" he puzzled. "Who is he? I don't know him."

The stranger beckoned again, his arm gesticulating rapidly and earnestly. His mind pounding with fear, Joseph gazed at the man not knowing how to respond. "Is he going to hurt me?" The impulse to run flashed through his mind but the man's face held him still. The stranger's footsteps crunched over the debris of the house as, stooping, he approached where Joseph was standing. Joseph's eyes were fixed on the stranger's face. Gentle but insistent he called to Joseph in a low, course whisper.

"Come this way. Quickly! Over here."

Again Joseph looked around with searching eyes. The closed faces of the neighbouring houses stared at him callously; he felt naked and exposed in the ruin of his home. The stranger was still urging him to follow as he crouched amongst the broken walls. With leaden feet, Joseph stepped towards the man, drawn by the kindness of his face. He had taken several wavering steps when the stranger sprang lightly up to him and stretched out his hands. Reeling from faintness, Joseph reached towards him and immediately the stranger took him in his strong arms and guided him out through the house, through the length of the garden, and into the brick shed that stood intact at the end of the garden.

The door scraped close, eclipsing the bright morning. Inside the cool darkness of the shed, Joseph sank wearily down and sat on the coarse wooden floor, leaning his back against the rough interior wall. His head hung despondently; his chest rose and fell with aching breaths.

The stranger's voice tumbled into the gloomy shadows. "I've made you some breakfast."

Joseph stared blinking into the dim light, his eyes straining through the shadows. A tall shadow stood leaning against the far wall. As Joseph peered intensely, the form of a man emerged from the gloom. The shadowy figure leant forward and with a snap, light suddenly burst into the room.

Joseph blinked with surprise. A small candle flickered precariously, sending dancing beams of light around the small space. Joseph gazed as his surroundings gradually emerged out of the darkness; first the soft contours of the stranger's face as he smiled gently, then the rough form of a table on which was laid a simple meal of bread and cheese and fruit. He turned his eyes around him expecting to see the usual jumble of tools, bikes, old prams, boxes and papers jammed in, but the shed appeared to have been cleared out and tidied. Instead it was furnished with two camping beds, piled with blankets, a small table, a small gas cooking ring and bottle perched on an old wooden crate, a few dishes and utensils, buckets and such like.

Joseph was still puzzling over the transformation of the garden shed when the man's voice broke into his thoughts. "Come and have something to eat, then you can sleep."

Mute and tired, Joseph crawled over to the table, and sitting on the floor he ate mouthfuls of bread and drank warm milk. His head sank lower and his mouthfuls grew slower as fatigue gradually overcame him. The man, who had been silently watching him eat, stepped carefully over to him, and lifting him gently, lowered him into one of the beds and smoothed the covers over him. Quietly, he tidied the food away, and sat down in the golden halo of candlelight to watch over the boy. Hours passed with only the flickering of the candle and the deep sighing breaths of Joseph, and the dark, shining eyes of the stranger watching protectively.

The stranger's eyes darted suddenly to the side as he sensed something moving in the dim corners of the shed. His body still and alert, he kept his gaze fixed on the area around the boy. He saw it move again. A low oily shadow that slinked and slithered its way towards the sleeping boy. The man waited, tense with anticipation. He heard the coarse whisper hissing seductively, wrapping itself around Joseph's dreaming mind.

The man's voice interrupted, sharp and clear. "What are you doing here?"

"What am I doing here?" the shadow hissed back angrily, "Shouldn't you ask yourself that question! This is my place now, remember. It doesn't belong to you anymore."

"I've come to take what's mine." The stranger's voice echoed back in tones of calm assurance.

"Yours! Ha! That's the point. There's nothing here that is yours. You're finished." The shadowy voice darted back with biting hostility. "They've all given themselves to me. All of them! It was so easy. Ha!"

"I've come to buy them back" The man's voice pressed on with a gentle certainty.

"Buy them!" The shadow shrieked hysterically. "Buy them with what, I ask?"

"With my life," was the short, simple response. "With my life."

The shadow was silent. The boy's breaths continued rhythmically. The shadow's voice was altered when it finally spoke again; rough and broken, tinged with apprehension, sobered with defeat. "So, who are you going to take?"

"As many as will come," was his quiet reply.

"Who were you talking to?" Joseph's boyish voice piped into the waiting silence.

"Hmm."

"You were talking to someone; I heard your voices." Joseph sat up, rubbing his stinging eyes.

The man's eyes followed the shadow as it shrunk back to the corner of the shed and hovered. Joseph looked around puzzled, searching vainly.

"Who's here? I can't see anyone." Joseph's small voice pressed anxiously.

The shadow smirked and expanded triumphantly.

"Away" The man's voice darted into the corner like a cannon blast. The shadow disappeared in a fraction of an instant. Joseph stared, startled and perplexed.

"You must beware of him. Keep right away from him. He will slide into your thoughts like dripping honey making you dream of chocolate and yawning in the sun; or chase you with terrors and anxious thoughts that circle your mind relentlessly. Make no room for him. None."

"But how can I keep away from him if I don't know who he is?" was Joseph's piqued reply.

"He is the one who made himself ruler of this land." The man's measured words pressed palpably into the circle of light that surrounded them. His voice was quiet but earnest." Out of envy, he stole what would have been given to him, if only he had loved."

Joseph's youthful eyes searched the lines of pain which creased the man's face. His voice continued heavily. "He has placed himself at the centre of his own reality and lives to serve himself. When he emptied himself of love he became hungry, with a hunger that he had never known. So, he rules in order to possess and control, rather than serve. He feeds on you all, infesting you with the same hunger; an insatiable longing to satisfy yourself with pleasure instead of love. That hunger is like a fear that drives everyone to have and control; to experience and achieve, or torments you with the terror of losing or not obtaining."

The man leant forward, fixing his gaze steadily on Joseph's wide eyes. "They are fragile people trying to sustain themselves on things that are made rather than on the source of life Himself. The brief sense of satisfaction evaporates like a mist and they are left, still hungry, still longing. They are trapped in a web they can't see."

The man's voice, swollen with sadness, paused. Joseph gazed deeply at his face as strong emotion wrestled with the man's gentle features. Candle-light leapt in golden ribbons which danced over his face
and threw waving shadows over the rough walls.

"So, how can I avoid him?" Joseph interrupted uncertainly.

"There is only one way to be safe from him. Stay close to me. Listen to every thing I say; take it into your mind and keep it dear; and do exactly what I tell you. Only I can release you from his influence; even you are caught."

"Me! How did I get caught?" Joseph questioned in surprise.

"When you doubted the truth and believed the lie."

"Doubted what truth?" Joseph retorted defensively.

"The deep truth that your father and mother knew; that they based their lives on."

Joseph started when he heard his parents mentioned. "You knew my parents?"

"Yes. I know your parents; and they know me."

Joseph squirmed uncomfortably to hear his parents spoken of, and as if they were alive. Pain stabbed in his chest and tears swelled in his eyes, breaking through the foggy cloud of numbness that had been protecting him. He slumped miserably and swam through the flooding stream of memories that deluged him.

"What truth did his father hold so dear?" he wondered. He strained to recall their last conversation. He trusted so much in the King that had made him and loved him. But the King hadn't stopped them burning his family alive. His mind ached with weary thoughts that confused him. He was starting to feel overwhelmed again. The man sensed it and beckoned to him.

"Come. Evening is soon falling. The streets will be quiet. We can go for a walk."

"Evening! What, have I slept all day?" Joseph asked in surprise.

"Almost. But there is still some light." The man, who had crossed to the door of the shed, dragged the door open admitting a narrow segment of light which stretched across the dusty floor to Joseph's feet.

Joseph clambered unsteadily upright and stepped out the door, blinking in the brightness of late afternoon. Dazed, he walked giddily towards the ruin of his home, but a hand grasped his elbow and pulled him back.

"Not that way," the man whispered, beckoning with his head towards the back fence at the end of the garden. "We'll have to be a bit less conspicuous."

Joseph let himself be dumbly led by the man as they climbed the fence and skirted their way through bits of woods and between gardens. They seemed to be making a great arc which made no sense to Joseph as they wove through lanes and crawled through bushes. Eventually, pressed behind the side of a fence, Joseph realised that he was actually back in his own street but on the opposite side of the road. He was just about to ask why, when he was met with a sharp "Shhhh".

Joseph and the man peered cautiously around the fence, being careful to not expose themselves. Joseph gasped and covered his mouth as he looked across at his own address. The smoking site was swarming with people. Uniformed men poked and turned things over, as they carefully examined and measured, scribbling notes and placing evidence into individual plastic bags.

Other officers tried to push back the wall of onlookers that were straining forward to see better. The crowd parted as a man shouldering a large T.V. camera forced his way through. A young woman with a flashing smile and swaying hair struggled to keep herself in front of the camera as the crowd jostled and elbowed her. Joseph strained to hear what she was saying into the large microphone that she was holding.

" ... the scene of tonight's tragedy ...a family and home destroyed in this terrible accident... experts are working just now to piece together the facts and pin-point the cause...to speak now to neighbour and friend, Mrs. Clyde, who was on the scene to witness this disaster... Mrs. Clyde, would you like to share with us your dreadful ordeal..."

"They were such a lovely family... of course I was the first to smell the smoke and I was on the phone to the emergency services right away; I rushed out and tried to do what I could, but it was too late, there was nothing anyone could do for them...It was just awful."

"Thank you Mrs.Clyde; now we have Police Detective Howe who will give us an update on the investigation."

"..most of the evidence at this stage would point to the conclusion that the fire originated in the kitchen and from this we can conclude that it was without doubt initiated by a cooking accident, from the grill or a pan of chips..."

Joseph groaned as he heard these painful lies being broadcast, and this crowd of people clucking over what good neighbours they had been. He held his breath as he watched two officers together wrench open the stubborn door to the shed and look inside. They withdrew after a brief look, shaking their heads sadly.

Puzzled, Joseph looked up to the man, but he seemed as calm as ever, and simply pressed his finger to his closed lips, indicating silence.

"...and so, it seems, sadly, that no-one has survived this tragic inferno, and there will be great mourning among this close community of friends and neighbours... this has been Jill Tyler for OTV news..."

The reporter pushed back through the crowd with her crew fighting to stay in her wake. Joseph watched her climb into a white van and followed her quick fingers as she snapped open a small vanity purse and dabbed briskly at her pouting mouth with lipstick, peering intensely at her reflection in the tiny mirror. The van swerved down the road and she glared irritatedly at the driver.

Joseph looked up at the man again. The man's eyes were moving over the scene; sweeping over groups, fixing on an individual, following someone else, taking in the whole, focusing on the particular. Joseph watched him intensely, wondering at the deep light in his eyes, the animation in his expression, every fibre of his face responding in recognition and love, misted with sadness and disappointment. Finally, his eyes rested on Joseph, meeting the boy's puzzled gaze.

"Shall we go?" the man softly whispered.

Joseph scanned the crowd of people swarming over the ruin of his home and nodded sadly. He turned and followed the man again as he weaved a winding path back through the patch-work of gardens, parks, lanes and woods.

When they stopped this time they had emerged in a quiet corner of the town square, sheltering behind the wall of the town hall. They stood with their backs pressed against the wall, still drenched in the late afternoon sun, and took deep breaths of warm air, filling their lungs and letting the air escape very slowly, their hearts still pounding from hurrying. Joseph waited till his breathing had slowed till he summoned up his voice.

"Why were all those people lying on television? It didn't happen the way they said at all."

The sun beat on their faces. Joseph screwed up his face and squinted to see if the man had heard his question. He was gazing languidly, as if lost in some thought. He turned and smiled at Joseph.

"They are so used to living a lie, they are not even aware of it any more. I don't think they even consciously lie, they are just not used to being fully honest. Before they have examined the real facts or their consciences, words are already pouring from their mouths, justifying, re-inventing, smoothing over; until the whole scene has been altered and laid down in their minds as a memory that seems real. It seems complicated but its actually so much easier than challenging yourself with the truth."

Joseph looked up surprised. To his child-like mind, a lie was a lie, and you may not want to admit it, but you know when you're wrong. The man saw his wounded face.

"Adults are so devious they don't know how much they are deceiving themselves. Come, let's have a wander around the shops."

"I thought we had to stay hidden?" Joseph questioned.

"Nobody will notice us here."

Joseph's mind reeled as he recalled the empty square and his father's voice lilting over the clatter of his footsteps. Now the square surged with a sea of people pressing their way from shop to shop. People streamed in a bobbing current down the length of the shop-lined arcades, pouring into the open shop-fronts; a tide washing over the glittery displays snatching up precious things before closure. Empty people engulfing things, swallowing them up hungrily; their faces painted with greed and a longing for more.

Joseph was swept along with the crowd, pressed by bodies pushing their way forward; carried nauseously through the steaming crush. He struggled uselessly against the crowd. Anxiety rose as he flailed helplessly. He strained to see through the shifting screen of shoppers, panic pressing in cold waves as he searched for the face of his man.

A firm hand grasped his arm and pulled him swiftly and surely from the streaming throng of people. As Joseph felt himself being pulled across the current of bodies he looked up into the face of his man. His gentle face was taut with anguish. Joseph watched his lips move but his words were lost in the clamour. As he drew clear of the noise he questioned the man. "What did you say?"

Grief swelled in his words which broke from him in hoarse sobs. "To think they gave me up for this. Gave up love for coloured plastic and shiny trinkets."

The boy stared, dumb with confusion but as tears filled the man's eyes he turned his gaze resolutely to the ground, stung with embarrassment. With head hanging, the man swung around and walked away from the crowd. Joseph hesitated briefly then galloped after him, panting as he drew alongside him.

The man turned his eyes down towards the boy as he took great strides across the square. "So, you still want to follow me?"

Joseph looked up confused and a little hurt. He stammered as he struggled to make his small voice heard. "Who else could I follow? I only have you."

The man stopped instantly on hearing the boy's words. Emotion drenched his face as he lowered himself to meet the boy's uncertain gaze. He looked intently into the boy's face for quite a time before speaking in a clear, low voice. "You have chosen very well. Bless you, you have chosen right." His hand grasped the boy's small shoulder and squeezed it with joy. His voice lowered seriously. "But it won't be an easy choice. The time will come when everyone will turn away from me and you might want to run with them. But if you hold on till the end..." His voice disappeared into a thin whisper of hope. "If you hold on ...oh, what you will see." He trembled with the vision that filled his mind and was unable to speak any more but wrapped his arms around the boy and drew him close. Joseph rested his head on the man's chest and felt the reassuring arms surrounding him. His heart quickened as it filled with a wonderful sense of hope.

"I think it's time for a proper tour of this old town and I'll show you what it says about me." The man loosened his hold on Joseph and with big strides again set off towards the Town Hall. "Have you ever been in here before, Joseph?"

Joseph gasped with surprise. "You know my name!"

"Of course I know your name. I know everyone's name. That is the least of the things I know. Now, did your good father ever bring you in here?"

"I think he did when I was little, but lately it has been too dangerous." Joseph's small voice began to tremble as he watched the man striding boldly up the Town Hall steps. "Do you think it's safe for us to be here?"

The man turned and looked down from the top of the flight of stairs which he had already scaled. "Nothing here is safe. Don't fear, just trust." He turned and continued his way into the massive portal of the hall.

Puzzled and fighting fear, Joseph mounted the stairs and ran after him.

Their footsteps echoed conspicuously as they stepped into the cool interior, the sun disappearing with a blink as the door closed behind them. A musty smell of old, damp stone met them like a pungent wave. Darkness hung around the periphery of the vast chamber.

"Is it not used any more?" the man questioned.

"Not since I can remember. They built new offices. The Commerce Centre is where everything goes on now." The boy's voice dropped. "It's considered pretty anti-government to come here. Enough to get you black-listed."

"Well," said the man in a buoyant voice, " I know why they don't want anyone to come in here." He pulled a torch out of his jacket pocket and indicated to the boy with a jerk of his head to follow.

With a mixture of fear and wonder, Joseph's eyes followed the yellow beam of light which streamed out of the man's torch and darted around the cavernous interior. "Now, let's find where it starts."

Joseph peered through the gloom to make out his surroundings. Beneath his feet stretched a great empty floor of huge flagstones worn smooth by the passage of people and time, and now littered with plaster debris, broken chunks of stone, smashed glass and twisted metal. Enclosing them rose imposing walls of gleaming white marble. High up the walls were interrupted by a row of windows, through which light streamed in fading beams. Finally, the towering walls met the fan-vaulted ceiling which domed the hall. As Joseph examined the hall, it was clear, despite the poor lighting, that attempts had been made to damage, even destroy, the interior. The windows were smashed and the ribs and ornate carvings of the roof were battered and broken; light fixtures and ornaments had been torn from the ceiling and walls and flung onto the floor.

The man moved silently around the hall searching with his torch.

"Hey!" Joseph shouted suddenly. "Do you notice something funny? Everything is wrecked except the walls. The walls are perfectly smooth, not even chipped."

"Of course," said the man quietly as he continued searching. "It's in these walls that I left my words. They couldn't destroy them."

Joseph looked at the man suspiciously. Confusion crossed his young brow as he wrestled with his thoughts. "But he's younger than my Dad and this hall has been here for centuries. He's not making sense."

"I know it's hard to understand." Joseph was startled out of his reverie by the man's steady voice and keen eye. "It will all become clearer soon. Right, here's where it starts." And following the small disc of light around the wall he began to read.

"He who has been since before the dawn of time, who always has been and always will be, He who is enthroned above all the universe, who rules in majesty and splendour and might, with justice, righteousness and love; He who is worthy of praise and is King and Lord. "

"Hang on," interrupted Joseph. "What are you reading? I can't see anything."

"That's because you're not looking. Come closer. Have a proper look."

Joseph stepped closer to the wall and leaned forward to examine the section of wall illuminated. Suddenly he exclaimed, "There is writing here!"

The smooth surface of marble was actually inscribed with fine lettering that wound in a long narration around the walls. Joseph continued reading. "Great is the King who is full of love and goodness; He is kind, merciful and compassionate. He is enthroned above; His palace is filled with love, joy and beauty. He is abundantly good and generous, and delights in giving gifts to all his people. He is worthy of love, honour and praise." Joseph broke off his reading.

"Why have you stopped?" the man asked.

"This sounds like the story Dad used to tell me."

"It is."

"How come he knew it?" Joseph puzzled.

"There was a time when everyone knew this story. Read on."

"The King wished to bestow special honour on His servant, one who was more beautiful and powerful than any other. He created a beautiful place; a town surrounded by fertile fields and woods, inhabited by good people, and placed His servant over it as governor, to rule it on His behalf. With a word it was all done. Every brick, stone and tree was in place and the King set His servant in its midst to give the people all the gifts the King had for them; love, peace, order, music, beauty, purpose, creativity and free-will. The town flourished with all its happy inhabitants, as did the servant who grew even more beautiful as he poured his own love and creativity into serving the people. Time passed peacefully and happily until something changed in the servant's heart. He became discontent with serving and wanted to be served. He became filled with thoughts about himself and lost his love. Pride and ambition consumed him and he rebelled against the King and made an enemy of himself. Since that time he has been working to turn the people against the King and to erase the memory of Him. By making themselves the centre of their own lives, the people have shown their allegiance to their governor and have alienated themselves from their creator. But the few that have remained faithful will be rewarded fully; they will see their King and Lord, and live with Him forever. At the right time He will come to redeem them, taking back to Himself all that is His. He that waits should watch carefully and know the sign of the true King who is coming, the King who gives himself up for His people."

"Is that it?" Joseph came to the end of the script. "Is it not going to tell me what the sign is?"

"You should know the sign, Joseph."

"Know it! How?"

"You're father told you."

"My father?" Joseph queried. "When?"

"During you're last walk together."

Joseph's thoughts ran back over the events of the painful evening. What had they talked about? It now seemed so far away and shrouded by the dismal fog that had overwhelmed his thoughts and feelings.

The man reminded him. "You asked your father how you would recognise the King when He came and he answered like this; 'He will reveal something that only a king could possibly have'."

Joseph jumped as he recognised his father's words. "How could you possibly know that?"

"That, Joseph, is what you have to work out."

Joseph stared in silence, deeply troubled by this strange man and the things he said and knew. The man's heart ached as he watched him struggling but he remained silent and watchful.

Suddenly the man's eyes darted sideways into the gloom. "Joseph, it's time for us to go."

Joseph was glad to leave the deserted building and felt a sense of relief as he pushed open the heavy doors and stepped into the bright evening light. He hurried to descend the flight of stairs feeling still too conspicuous. His eyes glanced around fearfully looking to see if he was being observed. The square was quieter now with the shops closing and the rush of shopping trailing away. No-one seemed to be looking his way. He shrank as he ran down, crouching into the balustrade to reduce his visibility and disappearing behind the wall at the bottom. The man walked casually down looking calmly around him. A dark shadow darted furtively behind him. The man looked over his shoulder briefly then resumed his steady descent of the stairs. The shadow moved again. "I know you're here," the man called out, "and I know what you're up to."

"Who were you talking to?" Joseph demanded when the man was at his side.

"Oh, just someone who is wanting to cause trouble," the man lightly replied.

"Oh no! Have we been seen? We shouldn't have gone in there."

"We needed to go in there. The trouble that is going to come to us must come, but it won't overwhelm us. And I have a plan." The man smiled reassuringly at Joseph who was pale with fright. "Just learn to trust me. I know what I'm doing."

As they moved away from the town hall the man turned to look over his shoulder and followed with his eyes a dark form that slid out of the shadows and cut across the square. A small group of children skipped and chanted in a singing game which wound in giggling loops and trains over the square. The figure glided noiselessly up and hovered at the edge of the game, weaving a lilting song which wound through the children's tune. Little heads turned and searched but most returned to their game. The song rose in stronger waves as the dark figure crooned and swayed. One little head turned and caught his hungry eyes; the girl's feet faltered and her own song died on her lips. With distracted steps she walked slowly away from her friends. To others watching she seemed to suddenly lose the thread of the game. They saw her pause as if listening intently, then lift her head to catch a boy and a strange man in her view. Without bidding farewell to her friends, she suddenly left, running.

The man walked on and Joseph followed. "Now, what does a king have that no-one else has."

Joseph thought. "Lots of money and jewels."

"Joseph, remember your little shopping expedition. There are plenty of people in this town dripping with riches and wealth, looking for more things to have. Try again."

"A palace?"

The man led Joseph up one of the streets leading off the square. "Look at these houses, Joseph. Think of some words to describe them."

Joseph looked perplexed. He looked up at the houses wondering what the man was wanting of him.

"Well, they're big." Joseph finally mumbled.

"Big!" the man exclaimed. "They're massive! Huge! Enormous! Palatial." The man's eyes met Joseph's. "Anyone with the resources can build a palace and put himself on a pedestal."

Joseph felt stupid. He was afraid to try again.

"Come on boy, don't be discouraged. You're learning to see and understand and that's hard. But don't give up."

The boy had a thought but it seemed childish.

"Come on," the man urged him, "just say it."

"A crown." Joseph kept his eyes on the ground expecting a rebuke.

"Yes. A crown. But what does the crown represent?"

"That he is the real king," Joseph answered tentatively.

"Good answer. And if he is the real king he has power and control. He has sovereignty. What is sovereignty?"

Joseph had never even heard the word before and shrugged his shoulders despondently. The man answered for him. "It is his authority to rule, to be in control in an overarching sense. We all exercise sovereignty over ourselves and our lives to a degree, but a king has sovereignty over all that belongs to him. If the king is also the maker, all that he has made belongs to him. This means the king has control over everything; the people, nature, the weather, history. Now, how might you see this sovereignty demonstrated?"

"By being able to make things happen the way he wants them to," Joseph projected.

"Yes. This king could take complete control over nature and history."

"And he could make everybody do what he wanted," the boy interjected excitedly, "and stop anybody from being bad."

"He could," the man admitted, "but what if this king wanted his subjects to be able to choose how they behaved? What if the king wanted obedience not because his subjects were obliged to or feared him, but because they loved him? What would he have to do?"

"I don't understand what you mean," Joseph faltered.

"This king wanted his subjects to obey him because they loved him not because they had no choice, so he gave them free will. That means they could choose to love and obey him, or they could turn away from the king and follow their own way."

"But then he might not see things going the way he wants them to," Joseph queried.

"Exactly. But as he is sovereign over history, this king has a plan, and a way to make everything turn out right in the end. Come, the time is drawing close."

The sun rested in a pink haze on the rooftops of the houses that lined the streets and thrust the pair into a dusky shadow as they walked in silence, each deep in their own thoughts. A voice startled them.

"Who's your friend, Joseph?"

Shaken with surprise, Joseph looked up into the face of a girl his own age. He stared dumbly as the girl stood twisting a plait through her fingers. "You weren't at school today. Where were you?"

Panic rushed through his mind as he struggled to answer. He looked helplessly to the man then back at the accusing eyes of the girl. Syllables floundered clumsily in his mouth but no explanation seemed possible. The man stood silent and still, his eyes fixed on the girl.

"Nothing to say?" The girl leaned forward with a malevolent smile, jutting her face rudely up to Joseph's. "Not surprised because I know where you went today and I'm going to tell."

Joseph's face blanched and his small body trembled with fear and agitation. The girl leaned back and crossed her arms with a look of victory on her unpleasant face. The man stretched out his arm to place his hand reassuringly on Joseph's shoulder. The girl's eyes slid up to his face which was warm with emotion but not fear. The deep kindness and compassion in his eyes pierced her like a spear. For a moment she wavered in her purpose as his knowing eyes searched her soul. She wrestled as their eyes remained connected then with a deep groan of anguish, she spun away and ran off, shouting, "I'll get you!"

The road wavered and tilted before him in a nauseous haze as Joseph staggered forward, retching and wheeling. Houses swam past in a blurred row and voices leaped towards him in jeering tones. Something was propelling him along the road, past the houses and faces that flashed past like a sickening dream. His ribs ached in a tight band as something gripped him, steering almost carrying him along. He looked sideways. It was the man looking ahead with determination, his arm grasping Joseph across the back and under his arm, almost lifting him as he guided him home. Joseph could hear the man's panting breaths and feel the rhythmic beat of their feet hitting the pavement as they jolted along, almost running. Fear and horror had overwhelmed Joseph's exhausted mind.

Finally Joseph felt the motion stop and with one strong kick he heard the wooden door scrape open. The man lowered Joseph onto his bed of blankets and seated himself beside him, his chest heaving with heavy breaths.

"What happened?" Joseph's voice bleated.

"You fainted. Just shock. You're O.K. now. Rest for a while. Put your head on the pillow and close your eyes. I'm going to make you something to eat."

Joseph let his heavy lids fall and in the darkness listened to the gentle sounds of the man preparing the meal. Stillness enveloped him as he started to float and dream. He was still running along the endless dark road trying to reach the fire. The faster he ran, the further the fire was from his reach. Tears were bursting in his throat drowning his voice as he tried to shout, "Dad!" Panic rose as he struggled to make a noise with his voice and his legs moved slower and slower as if he was being pushed back by some invisible wave of power. Then in the distance he saw his father standing before the flames. "Don't do it!" he tried to shout, but his voice was a hoarse whisper. His father was smiling and calling his name, "Joseph, Joseph." "Dad, don't do it."

"Joseph, Joseph. Wake up Joseph."

Joseph cautiously opened his eyes. The man was leaning over him. He stared up in confusion, terror still rushing through his blood. "It's you, not my Dad."

"Your Dad is gone now. He's safe now Joseph. They're all safe now."

Joseph stared in amazement. "You know where they are?"

The man nodded.

"Why didn't you tell me before?" Joseph sat up, hurt creeping into his voice.

"Would you have believed me before if I had told you I knew where they were?"

Joseph struggled, "Well, no."

"Do you believe me now?"

"Yes, I do."

The man passed him a bowl of steaming soup. He picked up his own bowl and began to eat, aware that the boy was watching him intently. "Eat your food; it will help you to feel better."

The boy took hesitant mouthfuls but his eyes were still fixed on the man.

"You have lots of questions, Joseph, and they will all be answered in time, but for now, eat and rest."

Joseph finished eating then curled up in his warm bed, aware of the sighing breaths of the man next to him. He waited till the light had been extinguished then let the tears he had been holding on to roll silently into the darkness. His body shook gently as emotion coursed in hot torrents, and ran in salty streams onto his pillow.

He felt a warm hand grasp his own. "I love them too."

"I'm afraid to close my eyes and see the flames again," Joseph blurted out.

"Then let me tell you where they are now. They are gathered around the table waiting for you to come so they can eat." The man's careful words tripped into the darkness, illuminating it with hope.

"But how can I get to them?" His small voice whispered.

Silence pressed against him as he waited with slow breaths.

"I will take you there," the man replied.

The boy felt peace spread through his heart and hugged the words in his mind for comfort until sleep drifted over him.

A beam of light shining through a crack in the shed wall stretched across Joseph's face and woke him.
He stared, wondering where he was and why he wasn't in his own bedroom. A noise disturbed him and he looked up to see the man cooking breakfast. He remembered and the reality was crushing.

"How did you sleep?" The man's voice called.

"Really well. I dreamed it all hadn't happened. I was with them in the kitchen. I was so happy." His voice faltered. "Why did it happen?"

The man paused and thought carefully. "Your father and mother know that the King is real and lived in obedience to Him. The King's enemies hated that and wanted to silence them, so they were killed." The man saw Joseph's young face crumple and quickly added, "They were killed but they are not still dead. As I told you, they are waiting for you."

"So how do I get to them?" Joseph enquired impatiently.

"Only the King can take you. And He will if you trust in Him. Here, eat this because there are some things we need to do today and it's almost time."

Joseph followed the man hesitantly as he eased his way through the doorway. He was surprised to see the man walk boldly through the blackened ruin and march onto the road in full view of the neighbours. Joseph picked his way across the rubble glancing suspiciously at the surrounding houses.

"Are we not hiding today?" he called apprehensively.

"No. Today is the time to be seen," the man boldly replied.

Joseph stared in amazement as he saw the man walk confidently out, waving to the curious faces that appeared from behind curtains and in doorways.

"Good morning Mrs. Lewis. The ring you have lost is in your apron pocket. You placed it there yesterday when you took it off to clean the bathroom." The gaping woman stared at him in amazement as her hand slid into her pocket. Pale and startled, she squealed in shock at her discovery, and held the ring up before her astounded eyes, grasped in her bony fingers.

" Mr Bryant," he addressed the man who stepped proudly through the next doorway, clasping a polished leather briefcase and fingering his tie. The suited man stopped and raised his eyes over his glinting spectacles defensively, arresting his gaze with a look of displeasure on the shabby man who's voice had surprised him.

"You're a lawyer, Mr Bryant. Is that not true?"

Mr Bryant seemed to inflate and broaden in reply, straightening up to reveal his full height, expanding his chest as if to encompass all that he had achieved. His eyes scanned his estate; imposing house in excellent condition, lawns manicured, flower beds tidy, expensive car gleaming before him. He bristled with satisfaction.

"A very successful lawyer, I believe," the man continued.

Mr Bryant could not deny it. He was not only successful but admired and respected.

"Would you say it was fitting for a man such as yourself; successful, respected; a man who upholds the law and defends justice; to be accepting a large gift of money in exchange for manipulating the law proceedings in your client's favour?"

The man's words crashed against Mr Bryant like an explosion; his face draining in shock. He stared unbelieving at the stranger as anger coursed through his flesh, replacing his surprise, and crimson surged through his puffed cheeks.

Broken words spluttered around his lips as he clenched his briefcase and strode aggressively towards his car, pushing past the man that continued to watch him carefully. The car engine stuttered and coughed under the trembling hands of its agitated owner, fumbling as he rushed to force the car out of view of the man.

The man followed the car silently with his eyes as it wove away, then continued along the road. Joseph followed at a flustered distance as he watched the man greet neighbours by name and astound them with personal comments.

Suddenly he stopped before a small cottage with the garden an untidy but pretty tangle of overgrown flowers, its walls nearly hid in a profusion of scented roses which climbed and rambled wildly. A small face darted into the shadow of a lace curtain. He stood patiently watching. Slowly the dark form of her face peeked shyly through the window. The man's face melted with love and his lips mouthed silent words to the young woman, "I know what he's doing to you. Hold on. I love you." Her face glistened with silvery trails, as pain poured through her wide, wavering eyes.

Her fingers pressed against the cold pain as she reached out towards him.

He continued on, his feet brisk, his attention everywhere. People eyed him suspiciously and hurried out of his way.

A youth turned abruptly out of his gate and pressed sharply up the street, his hands pushed deep into the pockets of his worn jeans, his face closed. The man crossed the road and began to follow him, his steps falling into the rhythm of the other's. The lad bristled uncomfortably and quickened his steps. The man outpaced him and drew closer until he was walking alongside him. The youth's head was turned sharply as he edged away, a shoulder hunched defensively. The lad came to a sudden stop and turned on the man with a barrage of violent language.

"Whatch ya doing, man. Clear off, or ...", the lad raised his fist threateningly.

The man met his eyes. "Don't go with those blokes; it will end in trouble. Keep away from them. They will be your ruin if you join them."

"What blokes?" the lad answered back rudely. "What do you know?" he asked defensively.

The man's voice continued calmly. "You know who I'm talking about. They're offering you money but they are just using you. They are no good."

The young man's face fell and his voice quavered desperately. "But I need money."

"I know," the man whispered soothingly, "I know. You are doing a fantastic job. It's not your fault that there's no money and no work. You're young to have the responsibility of a family but you're doing well.

Don't spoil it now. Don't be fooled by them. They are not going to help you."

The lad's face hung hopelessly. "How do you know?" he moaned.

"Am I right in the other details? Your Dad's run off, your Mum's sick and there are three young ones to look after."

The lad moved uncomfortably. "Have folk been speaking about us?"

"No. Folk are pretending you don't exist. Go back to them. Leave this crazy plan," he urged him. "Take this," he insisted, forcing a handful of folded notes into the boy's hand. "Believe me, work will turn up soon." He squeezed the lad's arm and continued walking along the pavement as the lad swivelled indecisively.

Joseph puffed up behind him. "Are you just making all that up?"

"Of course not, every word is true."

"But how can you know all those things?"

"That, Joseph, is the question you have to ask yourself."

Joseph trailed behind thoughtfully as the man strode ahead.

"Hurry up! We'll be late."

"Late for what?" Joseph mumbled to himself.

"You'll find out in a minute," the man called back. Joseph's face reddened as he realized the man had heard his offhand remark. He shuffled a little faster to catch up. They were approaching the town square at its busiest hour and the streets were teeming with people and cars.

Suddenly the man stopped. "Listen. In a minute you'll hear the car. Here it comes."

His Name is Love

Perplexed, Joseph strained his ears to hear a particular car over the general din of car engines and impatient hooting. He wondered what he was to listen for but it soon became obvious. He heard the screech of brakes and tyres as a car tore past them at a frightening speed, other cars swerving aside to avoid it.

"That's it. Come on now." The man resumed his pace. In a short while the man and boy were chilled by the sound of more screeching, a splintering smash and a heart-tearing scream. Sickness flooded the boy's mind.

"What's happened?"

"Don't worry," the man's voice was calm and soothing.

Joseph followed the man as he made his way through the pedestrians that coursed along the footpath. The further he went the busier the street grew. Ahead of them there appeared to be a crowd and more people were rushing towards the group. The sound of sobbing could be heard muffled by the mass of bodies. Then the sobs intensified into desperate wailing that tore at the hearts of all who heard it. The man grasped the boy's hand and began pushing his way through the crowd that was wailing and sobbing. The boy felt himself almost dragged through the wall of bodies that elbowed and stepped on him as they convulsed with grief. Finally, peering through gaps, he saw a horrifying scene. The wreck of a car was jammed into a bent street lamp, its driver was thrown forwards over the dashboard and was projecting through the shattered windscreen, and a distraught woman was clutching the lifeless and blood-strewn body of a child.

Joseph gasped in horror. The mother rocked back and forth with the child, groaning and wailing in anguish; blind to the crowd that pushed in around her.

The man gently parted the crowd and made his way to the woman. He kneeled down beside her, placing his hand on her shoulder. Joseph saw her shiver at his touch. Leaning towards her he spoke softly to her and her crying eased to gentle sobs. Slowly the mother placed her daughter in the man's arms. He took the small weight of the girl and lifted her carefully. In full view of the crowd he spoke to the dead child, "Wake up now," and the girl opened her eyes. The crowd contracted in a spasm of shock. The mother cried for joy, hugging her daughter, smothering her in kisses and tears. The child looked around perplexed and hid in her mother's arms from the crowd. The crowd switched from child to man in amazement, crying and laughing. Joseph shook with joy and clasped the man's hand fervently.

In all the noise and emotion , everyone had forgotten about the car and the driver, except the man who carefully moved across to the driver's door of the car and listened. A hush crept through the crowd as they observed him, hand on the driver's back, head bent low. In the quiet, soft groans and rasping breaths could be heard.

"Somebody call an ambulance," he shouted.

"Heal him yourself," somebody from the crowd called back.

The man made eye contact with the speaker. "You call an ambulance now."

The people were confused. They had just seen him raise a girl from the dead. Why wouldn't he heal this man? They watched the man leaning next to the driver, his lips moving incessantly with words of comfort and encouragement, his hand still resting on his back.

The crowd pulled away as the ambulance forced itself forward, and the paramedics jumped from the vehicle and rushed to attend the wounded young driver. The man gently stepped back still breathing his words of hope and strength. The ambulance officers expertly manoeuvred the driver onto a stretcher and wheeled him to the ambulance where they could commence treatment.

As he was moved away from the wreck of the car, the driver's eyes searched longingly for the man, scanning the crowd for a sight of him. The man stepped up to his stretcher and in a barely audible whisper the driver asked if the girl was alright. Tears of relief streamed down the driver's face as he saw the man nod and point to the entwined figures of mother and child. Another question troubled the driver as he struggled against overwhelming weakness and dimming consciousness. Ambulance officers were swarming with I.V. lines and dressings but he waved his arms feebly to brush them away. His eyes beckoned to the man and his failing voice called to him. The man placed his ear to the driver's moving lips, then looking at him squarely said in a clear voice, "You are forgiven."

An angry hum of indignation buzzed through the crowd as people glared in hot offence. Joseph watched as the man looked back at them, unwavered by their ill regard.

"Which of you will not forgive him? Is it you?" he asked looking straight into the tear-stained face of the child's mother. The woman's eyes trembled as she looked into the man's face.

"No." she murmured, caressing her daughter's hair. "I forgive him," she said glancing from her child to the bleeding driver.

"Is it you?" He crouched gently before the girl, his hand sliding around hers.

"No," she whispered, her smile lighting her warm cheeks.

"Well, who is it then?" The crowd shrank, cowering at his voice which boomed over them. He let the notes resonate and fade before he spoke again. "If you don't forgive him," he continued carefully, " then I shall not forgive...", he paused as he scanned the waiting crowd, his head moving slowly in an arc. His eyes stopped and rested on the face of a woman. Everyone turned slowly to look at a tall, well-dressed woman who's carefully made-up face and coiffured hair spoke of elegance and position. For an instant her head seemed to lift in subtle anticipation of admiration as the throng of eyes moved onto her. His voice resumed with certainty, "you, Ms Napier, for setting a gang of hoodlums onto this boy's family. They are all dead now, except him."

Eyes widened and flashed from the woman to Joseph. The woman's face flushed with colour as she stared back at the man violently, spluttering incomprehensibly, trembling with rage. Joseph jumped and bounced in his position near the man, straining to see over the crowd.

"Can you not see her, Joseph?" The man lifted Joseph so he could see the woman.

"I've never seen this boy in my life. I don't know what you mean," she blurted out venomously.

Joseph's small voice carried in clear tones tinged with dismay across the crowd of stunned listeners. "But I know you. You were my father's boss."

The crowd parted silently as the woman strutted away, her heels snapping conspicuously against the pavement. Joseph watched her solitary figure shrink as she moved further and further away and was lost in the distance.

Still caught up in the strong arms of the man, Joseph spoke softly to him. "She didn't like my Dad."

"No, Joseph. It was me she didn't like."

As the man gently lowered the boy to his feet, Joseph saw his face, lined with grief and pain.

"Are you crying for my father?" the boy enquired.

"There are no more tears for your father. He is home. It is her I am crying for because she will never come home."

"Why?"

"Because she loves it here too much and will never want to leave it." The man looked towards the place where the woman had disappeared into the crowd. "She has so much here," he continued sadly, "that she has no room in her heart for me." He looked down and smiled at Joseph. "And she doesn't know that what she has here is like tin, tarnished and worn-out, compared to the beauty I can give her. She is grasping onto a fragile happiness that sparkles for a moment in her hand, then crumbles and sifts through her fingers, vanishing with the wind." A quite radiance crept into his face. "She could have come to me and I would have given her joy like the rising sun which grows in spreading beams of warmth and light; like sunlight resting in your heart."

And as the man fell silent a hum of wonder spread through the crowd as they whispered to each other about what they had seen and heard.

Joseph watched the ambulance drive away and the crowd begin to drift apart. When the man turned silently to walk away, Joseph leapt after him, wondering where they were going. But it wasn't far. When they reached the square the man made his way across to the Town-Hall and sat on the steps. Joseph eyed the thin figure of the man sitting towards the bottom of this grand flight of marble, his elbows propped on his knees, his head resting heavily on his hands, staring out into the square which swarmed with people cutting back and forth across its expanse. The boy skipped up the few steps and dropped down beside him, unconsciously mimicking his pose. Heads turned cautiously towards them as people passed them, eyes darting up then quickly away. Joseph's body pulsed with apprehension as he peered at the watchful faces and furtive eyes. The man searched the square purposefully, his silent eyes moving slowly and intently.

"Here they come." Joseph started slightly as the man's voice broke the long silence. His eyes were fixed on a point at the far end of the square. Joseph strained but wasn't sure what the man was seeing. "Don't be alarmed at anything that happens today." His eyes remain fixed on the same point as he spoke. Fear surged through Joseph's pounding heart at the strangeness of the man's words. "When things seem to be going very badly, remember there is a plan."

In a sudden moment of passion the man turned to the boy with dark quivering eyes and gripped the boy's stooped shoulder's. "Tell me, Joseph, who do you think

I am?" The man trembled as he held the boy and looked into his face with deep searching eyes.

In an instant Joseph's heart leapt with the truth, and warmth crept through his cheeks as a glowing realization, but his lips stuttered in uncertainty.

The man urged the boy's gaping mouth, "Come on! You know it. Think of all you have seen and heard. Put it together."

The boy stared back silently. He had been studying every detail of this man as he had walked with him and he knew what all that he had seen and heard pointed to.

"You are the one spoken of in here." He gestured weakly towards the hall behind them, quivering slightly with the boldness of his assertion, but also with relief at having finally cemented his thoughts into words.

"You are the King". He looked back at the man, anxious for his response. The man's face shone with joy.

"You have spoken well, Joseph. Very well. Now don't forget it." The man glanced up away from Joseph's intent face and scanned the square. Looking back into the boy's eyes he said, "You need to hold onto what you know to be true with all your strength." The man's voice ended abruptly and he looked up. He quietly added, "They are here now."

Joseph looked up, surprised to see a small collection of people gathered at the foot of the stairs. With squinting eyes, Joseph peered at the milling group of people. He sifted through the faces, recognising some as neighbours, but most of them were strangers.

"Do you know them?" he whispered to the man.

"Yes. I know them all."

"Some of them look really angry. See how they're pointing at us. Why would they be pointing at us? Oh, there's the girl from the car accident and her mother. They seem to be arguing with the others."

The boy and man listened as individuals took sides in a heated argument, their faces taut with emotion, their fists waving with anger. As voices rose, people from the square were drawn closer to spectate. The man's eyes were moving carefully from face to face, studying them. The crowd jostled with men and women struggling against each other in passionate debate, while those on the periphery stretched and elbowed to get a view. Scattered amongst them were some that neither fought nor spectated but seemed to silently, impassively, intently observe, making a mental note of each person.

"Are you watching, Joseph?"

"Yes," the boy answered questioningly.

"Do you see him?"

"See who? I see lots of people," Joseph replied confused.

"Him. Wait till he moves. You'll see him then. There he goes. He slips like a shadow thinking I won't notice him." The man spoke with an abstracted tone as if his mind was preoccupied elsewhere.

Joseph stared carefully seeing only flushed faces and battling forms.

"See that man in the white shirt who's shouting now, well watch him."

Joseph focused on a man in the centre of the crowd who was red-faced with his vocal labours. "He lives in our street," said Joseph in the surprise of sudden recognition. As Joseph watched him, he gradually became aware of the form of a dark figure standing behind him. He peered at the shadowy figure as it crooned and whispered into the ears of the man. With a sickening sense of chill, Joseph realised that the dark voice was calling to him. His mind floundered with confusion and dread. He was filled with agitation and the longing to run away. "Why did this all have to happen? Everything was fine before and now it is a mess," he thought.

"It wasn't fine before." The man's voice broke into the anxious train of Joseph's thoughts. "He is confusing you; getting into your thoughts. You need to be sure, Joseph. Sure about what you have seen and heard; what you know to be true, because he will try to confuse you and rob you of all your hope. We don't have much time left. I am going to have to leave you soon, but you must believe that I am coming back for you." The man's eyes reached towards Joseph urging him to believe.

The crowd surged and wrestled like an angry sea, rude voices lashing against each other; the frenzy raged noisily around them but the boy sat in the stillness of the man's gentle voice and steady eyes.

"What do you mean you are leaving?" Joseph's voice started to tremble. "I don't want you to go away."

"I know, I know," the man whispered in soothing tones. "I have to; it's part of the plan. Remember that: it's part of the plan. You have to wait for me and try to recall everything I have told you. I love you."

"I love you" Joseph whispered back, and his voice disappeared into his constricted throat as he recalled his father saying the same words before he dived into the flames in his hopeless attempt to save the family.

"It's time." The man's voice was determined.

Joseph glanced up to see the crowd surging up the stairs, enveloping them. Joseph grasped the man's arm. He could hear the shrill, school-girl, telling-tales voice piping over the muddle and roar of arguments. He could hear the low, crooning voice winding through the words. He heard the official tones cough and commence, with just precision; "Now Miss, if you will just state clearly and precisely what you saw." He heard her shriek with hatred loosed in her voice.

"I saw him," she screamed, pointing her shaking outstretched finger to the pale, trembling form of Joseph, "I saw him in the Town Hall."

Silence fell heavily and cold on everyone as they stared at the boy and the pointing girl, frozen in her pose of accusation. No-one moved. Finally there came a cough and a stammer.

"Thank you Miss, that's all we need to know." There was a nod, a subtle gesture; a clearing of the throat; a calm, reasonable voice. "Young man you are arrested under the charge of Treason for unlawfully entering the Town Hall. You will be taken into custody to await trial." A wave of shock spread through the onlookers. Two men stepped skilfully to each side of the boy and grasped his arms securely. The boy hung limp and small within their hold. Bewildered, he turned to the man, his eyes pleading silently.

The man smiled and whispered, "Remember the plan". The crowd seemed suspended in amazement, choked with surprise.

The man's voice broke into the pressing silence with clear, strong words. "Release him. It is me you want."

The boy's face darted up with pain. "No."

The officials mumbled, confused and stuttered in contradiction. "I have on evidence from the witness that it was the boy."

The hissing voice rose in agitation from the darkness. "Take him, take him."

The official blushed and hesitated, mumbling under his breath. "Take the boy?"

"No, not the boy," the foul voice almost screamed in agitation. "The man, take the man."

The official squirmed uncomfortably. He jerked his head in a signal to his men, who released the shaking boy, and took hold of the man instead, dragging him roughly down the stairs, through the gaping crowd and across the square.

Joseph sank down onto the hard, cold stone step, his mind reeling, his body weak and trembling. He watched the figure of his man shrink and disappear as he was marched across the square and into a waiting police van. The city seemed to stretch vast and empty around him as he sat alone, oblivious to the people surrounding him. The weight of despair pressed heavily against him, numbing his mind, crushing his small heart. He sat frozen as one by one the people, who had, only moments before, been a heaving, contentious crowd, left and resumed their purpose. Joseph was only dimly aware of them leaving; distantly aware of the steps being emptied as his mind followed his man.

A gentle voice called to him. Her voice was like a distant dream washing against his wakening mind. The warmth of her hand touched him like breath on a frozen window pain. He slowly became aware of her small fingers nudging the cold flesh of his arm, calling.

"Joseph, Joseph."

He turned his head slowly and her small face was smiling into his with sparkling eyes. It was the little girl from the car accident, and her mother; the only ones left standing on the steps. They were both smiling down at him. Joseph stared back at them blankly.

"Why don't you come home with us?" The mother's words wove reassuringly through the boy's mind.

She bent down and lifted Joseph by the arm and led him away from the town centre.

VII

Joseph cried soft tears as he sat in the warm kitchen hugging his knees as he perched on a chair watching the mother prepare toast and warm milk. The little girl leaned on the table beside him watching him intently. The mother's voice floated around the kitchen in peels of homely conversation but Joseph was only half listening, his thoughts filled with the morning's events and the image of his man being led away. Food appeared before him and he ate distractedly, aware of the girl's eyes hovering over him.

The mother eased herself into the chair opposite, cupping her hot tea in her hands and sipping slowly. Silence fell over the kitchen as Joseph slowly chewed his toast and watched the curls of steam rise from the teacup. The silence stretched into awkwardness. The girl still gazed with fixed eyes.

The mother looked down and coughed nervously. "So, is he the one we have been waiting for?"

Joseph choked with surprise. He coughed and spluttered, trying to clear his throat, his mind an uproar of frantic thoughts. He gulped his milk to calm his convulsing throat, his mind whirling with answers to the question.

"Don't panic, Joseph," the mother's voice was steady and reassuring. "Just reflect slowly on what you know about him."

Joseph struggled to control his leaping thoughts and fears, and recalled the last words the man had shared with him in those fleeting moments on the steps before chaos had enveloped them. The man had asked him the same question, "Who do you say I am?" Joseph thought back through the last days of being with his man, of the things he had said and done, of the things he seemed to know. He thought of the words inscribed around the walls of the town hall, the same words that were wound through all his recollections of home and family and rang like a song through his heart. He looked up from his thoughts and saw the mother and girl waiting on him determinedly, smiling with expectation. Apprehension seized him, with the burden of speaking truthfully.

The mother observed his anxious face. "Take your time, Joseph. Just think through the facts clearly; don't let your feelings get in the way."

Joseph's fears tumbled through his mind like a gushing stream. "Is it true, or do I just want it to be true? Am I making it seem real because I want it to be true? How can I know?"

The little girl stretched out her hand and curled her fingers around Joseph's pale, cold hands. Joseph felt the warmth from her tiny pink hands creep into his icy flesh and press back the coldness that was enveloping him. He looked at her rosy face and remembered her, pale and lifeless, hanging limply in her mother's arms. The reality startled him. "Everything is happening exactly as he said it would."

The mother smiled at his sudden exclamation.

"He is the King," Joseph said jubilantly. "He is the King." He paused thoughtfully, "If he is the King he must be coming back. We must wait for him." And as the shadows deepened and stretched across the room, sunlight glowed in Joseph's voice as he retold all that had happened. And as he spoke he felt his heart expand with hope and trust.

VIII.

Joseph hurried across the square nervously looking around him, conscious of everyone who noticed him; aware of the people who stared in recognition, and of the people who distrustfully looked away. He stopped by a Newsagent to read the headlines; black ink sprawled boldly across the flapping sheet of paper: "Man on trial for treason". He darted into the shop to buy the paper, followed by dark, reproachful looks. He skirted back around the square and disappeared into the network of small streets that circled the centre.

As he made his way back to the house of the mother who had taken him in, he sensed movement behind him. With a pricking sense of dread, he looked around and saw a man some distance away. Joseph pushed himself to walk faster, anxiety growing in nauseous waves. He darted into a lane and continued briskly, but soon he heard the man's steps close behind him. Straining to steady his racing heart, he turned quickly and scuttled up a side street. Still the following footsteps snapped close behind him. As fear gripped him, Joseph began to run in blind panic, rushing towards his new home. As he hurried he heard the man pressing behind him, his steps beating the pavement, his breaths panting in short gasps.

"Boy," he heard the man call between breaths. In a rush of terror, Joseph sprinted up to the house and threw himself against the door, pounding it for entrance. He battered the door trying to force it to open as the man drew closer. The door was finally opened by the mother who looked up and down the street in bewilderment as Joseph threw himself inside. She was just about to shut the door when she heard a small voice and noticed the man steadying himself as he regained his breath.

"Madam," he gasped, "can you tell me about this man who brings the dead back to life."

The mother examined the man as he leant against the gate-post, pulling with one hand at his tie and shirt buttons to loosen them around his steaming neck. He was maybe thirty or forty, his suit a little dishevelled from running, his dark hair falling across his forehead. She searched his face cautiously, then looking around beckoned with her head for him to enter. She ushered him into the hall, closing the door behind him and quivering with alarm, she spoke in a hushed voice.

"How do you know about such a man?"

"It's written that such a man will come and free us," he whispered in a low voice, "and I have heard what the people are saying, that a girl was brought back to life. Is it true?"

"Why do you come asking me?" the mother questioned him.

"Because of the boy. Everyone says that the boy was with him before he was arrested. I tried to speak with the boy but he was too afraid."

The woman fixed her eyes on him again examining him for truth. The man shifted uncomfortably under her gaze.

"I know you are afraid of me too. I'm sorry, I shouldn't have come here. Please excuse me," the man mumbled sadly as he moved to leave.

"Wait," the mother's voice arrested him. "How did you hear of the man?"

"My mother told me the stories when I was a boy. She said I should wait for him to come." The man lowered his face which was clouded with emotion. His voice continued uncertainly, "She was taken away years ago and I haven't seen her since. I have been trying to live as if the King didn't exist, making money, living for myself, keeping out of trouble; but as soon as I heard about this man, I knew he was the one my mother had spoken about." The man became more agitated. "I have to know. It's become unbearable, not knowing."

The mother reached out her hand in comfort, soothing his trembling body. "Stay," she insisted, as he made to leave. "Stay and talk for a little while. What's your name?"

"Mark. Mark Hamilton," he answered hesitatingly, searching her face, squirming in his vulnerability.

She smiled and led him along the narrow hall into the warm kitchen where Joseph had retreated. She saw the boy shrink away as they entered. "Its O.K. Joseph. He won't hurt you. He wants to know about the King."

The mother turned to fill the kettle as the man and the boy looked at each other awkwardly. "Tell him Joseph. He wants to know if your man is the one in the stories. Is he?"

Joseph looked up at the man in fear, memories leaping through his mind. "I think he is," piped his small school-boy voice.

Silence filled the room as the man stood awkwardly in the doorway and the mother made tea.

"Why don't you sit down? she said, placing a cup on the table before him.

He lowered himself into a chair and leant over the table, sighing deeply. "But how can you be sure?"

"For lots of reasons; for lots of things he said and did. But mostly because of the way he loved me." Joseph slid the paper across to the man. On the front page beamed the gloomy headlines. "It was me they arrested, but he insisted that they take him instead." The boy trembled as he tried to speak. He continued in a whisper. "They want to kill him." His voice broke off.

The room fell silent except for the soft sound of tea being sipped, and the chink of china as cups settled in their saucers.

"Any way," Joseph's voice rose out of his troubled thoughts, "they won't be able to kill him because he said he has a plan and I'm to wait for him." After a pause he continued. "He said he's going to take me to where my family is, so he can't die. He must have an escape plan." His voice rose with hope. "That must be what he meant by a plan; an escape plan."

The adults exchanged concerned looks across the table. "Joseph, your man is in serious trouble; the law is powerful. They mean to kill him." The mother's voice broke off.

Joseph looked up offended. "You don't believe that he is the one." Joseph's voice was stretched with hurt.

"That's not true. I just don't want you to be let down if they succeed in killing him. You don't know what they are like."

"I know what they are like; they killed my family." His hurt voice stopped abruptly.

Silence enveloped them as they sat with lowered eyes and burning cheeks, shifting awkwardly and drinking their tea.

The strange man's voice broke uncertainly into the heavy silence. "And mine," he added solemnly.

"Yours?" Joseph gasped.

The man nodded as he bent forward under the weight of his grief, his hands covering his lowered face, his chest heaving with anguished sighs. "I betrayed them. I betrayed him," he groaned.

Her young voice rang with singing sweetness over the heavy dirge of emotion; her words unfolding like a spring flower. "Look at me; I was dead but he gave me new life."

As the sunlight slanted in through the window and cut across the gloom of the room, the little girl twirled her fairy form in a dance, catching the golden beams in her bright hair; her cheeks flushed with rose.

His Name is Love

IX.

Joseph sat on the marble stairs and stared pensively across the square; searching. Figures moved busily back and forth, but he couldn't see the figure he was looking for. His eyes squinted in the glaring sun as he imagined the form of his man emerging from the jumble of zigzagging people and walking up to him with his broad smile. In his mind he recalled his blue shirt and jeans, his dark hair cropped roughly, the deep pools of his eyes. He scanned the crowd for the right colour blue, the right build of man, the right swinging gait. The figures swam in the white sun as his burning eyes smarted and were rimmed with salty tears. He was a small figure perched compactly in a sweeping expanse of white stone and marble; a dot amongst the rising tiers of architecture; insignificant amidst the relentless pursuit of commerce. His mind grew heavy and slow, as the sounds of the crowded square receded into a distant hum.

A flash of blue darted past his sleepy eyes; like a gust of cold wind it startled him into wakefulness. His heart thumping, he searched intently. He found the blue; the right blue shirt. He stood up; alert, anticipating. The figure was a man's; it was moving towards him; emerging from the crowd and moving towards the stairs. Joseph had known his man would come back to the stairs. He leaned forward to see the man. The figure was limping. Joseph recoiled in shock; was his man hurt? Pain clung to his heart as he walked down the steps, eyes fixed on the man. The man got closer. Disappointment flooded Joseph's mind; it was not him. It was someone else; not the man he was waiting for.

Joseph stopped and with dismay, sank down onto the steps, his eyes still following the man.

It was the wrong man but he was still making his limping way towards Joseph. Joseph's face was creased with concentration as he watched the man make a direct path towards him. The man struggled painfully to the foot of the steps and called. "Can I speak with you?"

Joseph gaped uncertainly and looked around. The man continued to stare at him.

"With me?" he mouthed. The man nodded.

Hesitantly, he walked down and stood in front of the man. The man's faced was lined with fine scars, of partly healed lacerations. He winced as he moved, as if in pain. Joseph looked at him, puzzled, and waited for him to speak.

"Do you know who I am?" he asked finally.

Joseph searched his memory. "No."

"Do you not remember witnessing a car crash recently?"

Joseph felt his startled heart surge. "Were you...?"

"Yes, I was. It was me that drove a car into that little girl." His voice quivered and his face darkened with emotion.

"She's alright," Joseph's little voice piped optimistically. "She's better. Quite fine."

"I know. He told me. He said that she had died, but he had brought her back to life. Did this really happen?"

Joseph nodded his head slowly. "It did. I saw it."

Light seemed to grow in the man's eyes. "And where is he now, this man? He said so many beautiful things to me; I want to hear him speak again."

Joseph's face darkened and twitched with emotion. His heart writhed as he attempted to speak.

"But you were with him, weren't you? You know how to find him." The man pressed him earnestly.

"They took him." Joseph squeezed his words out painfully.

"Who took him?" The man's voice was stretched with agitation.

Joseph passed him the newspaper he was holding and pointed to the small article reporting that his man had been found guilty of treason and was awaiting sentence.

The man's face blanched as his eyes quickly scanned the print, jumping urgently from word to word. He finally stopped and looked up, his eyes wide in horror. "But this can't be true. Everything he said...I thought... that he was the one, the King."

"He is," Joseph retorted firmly. "He is the King and he is coming back for me. He said I should wait for him so that's what I'm going to do."

The man stared dumbly, disturbed by the news, confounded by the boy's obstinacy.

"But if he's been arrested and tried, and found guilty...he has no hope. They'll kill him."

"He's going to escape." Joseph retorted sharply.

The man's eyebrows leapt upwards. "Escape!"

"Yes" replied Joseph, finally.

Suddenly a rabble was running towards them, shouting and waving their arms. "Hey! You there. You are the one who was with that man who calls himself the King."

Joseph and the man looked up as they saw a dozen or so men rushing toward them, shouting in rude and angry voices. Instantly, the man turned and started hurrying away, hobbling painfully. Joseph was frozen in confusion.

"Run," the man called back as he limped out of the square. The angry horde of men drew closer but Joseph's legs were cold with dread and indecision; he couldn't move.

In a sudden moment of panic, Joseph found himself running as fast as he could up the stairs, scaling the wide marble steps two at a time as he bounded up, away from the crowd. Breathless he paused at the top and looked down over the heads of the men as they puffed and panted their slow way up the climb.

In another unmeditated moment, he found his voice ringing over the square, arresting the crowd, "He is the King." And as he saw the crowd grow in fury, he ran into the Town Hall, pushing the heavy doors close behind him. He stood in the dim light listening to heavy footsteps slap against the stone steps as they ran up in pursuit. Bewildered, Joseph looked around for some way of barricading himself in, his eyes straining to see anything with the sudden loss of light. Anxious seconds throbbed with fear as his startled eyes searched the gloom, details emerging too slowly.

"Bolts! The door has bolts." He frantically wrestled with the rusty metal bars that scraped and creaked as he tried to move them. With great effort he managed to work one bolt into place, but he could hear the shouting crowd approaching noisily and his fingers stumbled clumsily as he tried desperately to move another bolt.

He heard the stamping feet and jeering voices rise in a crescendo as bodies flew against the door, pounding the timber with their fury, heaving with anger and determination. Joseph edged back from the groaning door in horror, waiting for the timbers to splinter and burst and the mob to come spewing in over its ruins.

He shrank into a huddle with his ears covered, watching for the first violent foot or fist to reach him. The hall echoed with the onslaught. Joseph crouched with wide frightened eyes.

The door received the battering with an impenetrable thud; the pounding and hammering of fists and fury beat against it, flesh pounded into its frame, but it remained closed. The noise shook the walls but the door did not give way. Joseph stared in wonder as the door held its place against the rampage. He could hear the anger and frustration grow outside as they battered the door with all their force.

Joseph clutched his ears as beat after beat the door was struck, but it showed no sign of opening. Eventually the sounds grew less frequent and the rumble of voices drifted away. Silence crept into the hall as the voices moved further and further away, and grew to fill the dim space that stretched around him. Joseph remained hugging his knees, trembling.

There was solace in the stillness and half-light that hovered around him, blanketing his sorrow, soothing his sharp breaths. Nothing moved but a narrow band of sunlight that stole in through the high windows and slowly crept across the breadth of the dusty hall, casting a beam of brilliance into the gloom. Joseph huddled into the darkness with closed eyes and clenched limbs. Slowly the light inched towards him, scattering the shadowy light. Warmth crept into the boy's back as the sun spread across his folded body, stretching up to his bent neck. He shivered as the heat fell across his bare skin. Startled, he opened his eyes to find himself bathed in warmth and light.

Joseph stood up and looked around him, blinking. The marble walls of the hall were crowned with windows that glinted with splintered glass. Joseph followed the row of windows as it wound around the perimeter of the hall. Suddenly he came across a stone balcony that stretched across one end of the hall, just beneath the high row of windows. Spiralling down from the balcony was the twisted and battered remains of a metal staircase. Joseph hurried to it, driven by the pressing desire to look out of the windows. He scrambled and climbed up the bent and dangling metal bars, eventually pulling himself up onto the balcony. Joseph made straight for the windows that overlooked the square, leaning forward to peer out through the shattered panes of glass.

Beneath him he could see the steps falling away in a glistening sweep of white. They were empty now. Beyond them the square spread out, strangely still, the people crowded to the far end, gathered expectantly. Everything was unusually quiet except for the distant sound of hammering. Joseph strained to make out what was happening. Above the heads of the people a wooden structure was slowly appearing as heavy beams were hoisted upright in jerky movements. Joseph blinked in horror as he began to recognise what it was that was being heaved and hammered into place. It was like a rough frame of wood standing on a platform, but from the centre of it swung a thick, curling length of rope.

Joseph remained pressed against the cold stone wall of the balcony as the sun inched its way across the square, elongating the shadows as time passed into the afternoon. His body was stretched so his small face could peep over the high wall; his eyes fixed on the gallows that rose out of the sea of people that now massed in the square. His body numb and cold with waiting, Joseph watched intently. The hours were filled with agony.

Finally the stir and moving of people flickered across his glazed view. Adrenaline surged through his body as he stretched further to see more. He could see the crowd parting to admit a procession, and swallowing up behind as the group passed through. Joseph watched the small figures make their way towards the platform and flow up the stairs. As they assembled across the small stage, Joseph saw the figure he had been looking for all these days. His heart beat painfully as he recognised the form of his man. Fear stabbed anxiously as the man was separated from the others and pushed roughly towards the centre of the platform. Joseph was frantic with distress as he watched, powerless and silent, while men looped the rope around his neck.

As Joseph watched in horror he felt the eyes of the condemned man slowly and deliberately turn onto him. Despite his smallness as he stretched just to see over the stone wall, and his distance as he perched in this high window, Joseph felt the man's eyes meet his and hold him in the strength and purity of his gaze. The man's eyes fastened onto him like an embrace of pure love that gripped his small frame and filled him with warmth. His eyes continued to hold him as the crowd jeered and shouted at him, waving fists violently; as one of the government officials on the platform read out his sentence; and as a thuggish man tightened the coarse rope around his thin neck. Silence fell over the square as the party left the platform in solemn procession, descending into the crowd.

The boy's eyes streamed with tears as he watched the man standing alone. Joseph saw the man's lips moving; he was speaking to the crowd. He was speaking to them in soft tones of love, of invitation. Joseph strained to see his lips moving, to discern what he was telling them. As his eyes followed the man's lips, somehow the boy understood; understood the call to go with him, be with him for ever, to join him in his kingdom. The crowd became frenzied with laughter and abuse; hurling insults and rejection at him; screeching with hate. Still love and compassion poured out from the man as the crowd gyrated in anger.

Squinting down at the scene, Joseph caught a glimpse of a slinking dark shadow curl like a foul fume through the heaving mass of bodies. He searched and it had gone. Again he saw it move, lapping at the feet of the man as he stood alone on the wooden scaffolding. His voice hissed and crooned. "I don't think anybody wants to come with you. I think they are all very happy here with me. What a shame. What a waste. You have gone this far and you will have to die, but you'll have no-one to take with you. They are all mine." His laughter hissed and cackled as he seeped away like oil, disappearing into the crowd. Joseph boiled at the injustice; the ugly, lying words tore at his love and eroded his silence. His passion exploded within him and in a moment his voice rocketed powerfully from his sanctuary.

"You are wrong," the boy's voice bellowed across the square. "All your words are filthy lies," his words echoed from the stucco-faced buildings and burst into the crowd. "There is someone who will go with him; who wants to be with him in his kingdom. Me!"

The crowd searched around them to see where the voice was coming from. The man smiled with glowing eyes. The shadow contracted into a form and whispered maliciously, leaning malevolently into the circle of officials, directing their darting eyes, manoeuvring their alarmed thoughts. "It's time," he pressed, "Do it now."

"It's time," the man mouthed to Joseph. "Don't be afraid."

The boy heard the timber creak, saw the rope twitch taut and the man writhe. In a second it was done; finished. The world seemed frozen, for a moment immobile, its breath expended, its life gone. A grave pause. The crowd murmured with confused emotion, awkwardly trying to shake off the unexpected impact. Movement stirred through the numb crowd, waking them from their shock. His body hung crumpled and empty before them, swinging slightly from the jerk as they stood staring.

Boots snapped nastily against the hard ground as a dark figure separated from the gaping crowd and strode aggressively towards the steps of the platform. From his distant perch, Joseph saw a uniformed man sweep coldly up the stairs and in one bold movement, draw a sword from his waist and plunge it deeply into the chest of the lifeless man. Groans burst out from the reeling crowd as blood sprayed in a torrent and poured onto the ground. People leapt back in horror, shoving each other as they fought to stay clear of the stream of blood which was spreading across the cobblestones, forming rivers that coursed dangerously along the ruts. In screaming confusion figures ran chaotically from the square which quickly emptied and fell into silence.

The boy gripped the cold stone wall in his icy fingers,

staring at the place the man had been. One painful thought gripped his heart; "He died instead of me."

X.

Lightening bursts through the endless reaches of the universe with terrifying grandeur; fire raging across the skies like a storm. The multitude gaze with shining eyes and held breath. Gleaming figures approach each other across the surging sea of light, flames leaping from their drawn swords. One shines like the midday sun, with the radiance of precious jewels, carnelian and jasper, His eyes like blazing fire, His head adorned with crowns. He is dazzling gold, the sun amongst the brightest stars.

The other is wrapped in garments of fading light as he clings to his beauty which is slipping away; his goodness lost. He grasps his shining robes as they slip from his shoulder, revealing a glimpse of the darkness beneath. His head is circled in counterfeit foil, his pride masquerading as glory.

The heavens roar as they draw near for combat; the sun standing in the pure light of His purpose; the fading star dancing around Him in a desperate show.

Words issue from His mouth like a shining stream of burnished steel; a sword arising from His heart and plunging into his opponent. The little star is hurled down by the strength of his words; the truth burning like sulphur in his black soul.

Trembling with anger, his garments of light cast aside, he gathers his evil intent to himself, bloating himself on revenge. Clenching his ugly sword of destruction he sneaks like a dirty shadow towards the feet of his Lord. The multitude gasp with dismay; their voices resound with shrill alarm.

The King's eyes burn with steady fire, watching; all

seeing; all knowing; light reflecting off every detail. The voices rise in fervent warning. He sees, He knows; He waits; He is still.

The darkness lurks towards Him, cowering in His burning light, and lunges desperately; waving his sword dangerously before him; striking at the King's glowing feet.

All heaven contracts in a spasm of horrified grief; a groan which echoes through the myriads of shining beings. Scarlet blood spurts from His gaping heel and streaks His white robes in crimson; blood which pours into streams and pools, for the washing of the nations.

The evil one crouches in smirking satisfaction, basking in the horror. The King writhes in the anguish of searing pain; agony grips His soul. The multitude are silent; aghast.

Time pauses as heaven and earth cease their motion, emptied of life, silent.

In a slow deliberate movement the King tightens His fingers around the hilt of His sword and raises it above His head. Flames of light streak through the heavens in ruby and turquoise. His sword cuts a decisive arc as it rushes towards the ground, slashing through the deceiver, severing his head in a stroke. Devouring flames engulf his lifeless body.

As one breath the multitude inhale and pour out their love in song; the joy of their hearts entwined in tunes that swell at their Saviour's feet, lifting Him into the highest reaches of heaven, ringing with His glory.

XI

The fiery ball of sun dipped behind the rooftops and the square fell into deep, cold shadow. No footsteps crossed the cobbled ground; the last pigeon flapped noisily up to its retreat in the high eaves. Joseph continued to stare into the desolate night, as the shadows merged and filled the town. The man's body hung pale and cold as darkness closed around him. An unnatural silence had spread over the town, muting the twilight sounds. A cool breath of wind rushed over Joseph, making him shiver, stirring his mind. He heard the air whisper as it rushed through the broken window panes. It spoke to him like a voice. Alarm raced through his skin.

"Joseph," the voice called again. He jumped in shock as a stone whistled past his face and cracked against the stone wall nearby.

Terrified, Joseph peeked over the window ledge and looked down. He could see a figure vaguely in the shadows below. The voice called again in a hoarse whisper, "Joseph."

Joseph could not make out who it was. He leant over cautiously. "Yes," his voice finally answered. He stared at the white oval of face that looked up at him. It seemed to be a man.

"We need your help," the man called back.

"Who are you?" Joseph asked timorously.

Another figure appeared beside him and answered.

"Joseph, it's me," a woman's voice called up to him gently. Joseph recognized the voice of the girl's mother.

"Is it you?" he breathed his answer, almost in a whisper.

She caught his words and reassured him. "Come down, Joseph, it's us, your friends."

"And his friends?" Joseph questioned suspiciously.

"Come down, Joseph, and we'll talk."

Joseph stared at the figures almost lost in the gloom. Doubt and mistrust battled with his mind, but he was cold and hungry, swaying with tiredness. With a crashing sense of sick hopelessness, he stiffly clambered down from the balcony and shuffled through the darkness, looking for the door.

As his eyes adjusted to the interior he had the strange sense of a luminous light growing around him. He looked around for a light source. Slowly he became aware that the faint light was coming from the walls. Joseph staggered towards the walls with outstretched arms, tripping over the rubble and debris that was scattered over the floor, squinting his eyes in concentration. The boy blinked his smarting eyes as he drew nearer to the strange, luminous walls. He pushed his face closer and closer, till he discovered the reason for the light. It was the words inscribed in the smooth walls that were glowing clearly in the darkness.

"He came not to be served but to serve, and to give his life as a ransom for many."

Joseph re-read the verse to himself and pondered, his young brow crossed with confusion.

A bang on the door startled him. Cold shock surged through his weary body.

"Joseph." The rough whisper reached through the gloom. "Unlock the door; it's us. Joseph, are you there?"

Joseph staggered across to the door and wrestled the bolts free with his numb fingers. The door swung open and revealed a small group of figures huddled in the shadows. The mother stepped forward and wrapped her arms around Joseph's small, shivering form. Quickly, she and two others darted inside the hall and closed the door. She looked carefully at Joseph's pale, exhausted face.

"You're cold and hungry." She smoothed his cheek with her motherly hand. Reaching into a bag she was carrying she pulled out a coat and helped Joseph into it, then she passed him a bag of food.

"Eat; you'll feel better."

Joseph shook with relief and emotion as he pulled the coat over his shivering body and drew sandwiches out of the bag. He looked up at the other faces struggling to recognise them in the shadows. One was the man from the car accident, who he had last seen limping out of the square; the other was the man who had followed him home. They both smiled at him from under the dark hoods they had pulled over their heads. They sat in silence listening to the sound of Joseph chewing hungrily.

Finally his small voice broke into the silence. "Is it you, Mark?"

The man nodded.

"And you are still with us."

He nodded again. "Are you alright, boy?" Mark whispered with tenderness. "Did you see it happen?"

Joseph nodded and his face fell as silence gripped the group again. Minutes passed before Joseph spoke again.

"I don't know your name." he said to the man from the accident.

"Peter," his soft voice replied. He paused with his face lowered to the ground. "I'm sorry that I ran off and left you there, in the square earlier. I panicked when I saw everyone running for us. Can you forgive me?"

Joseph looked at him uncertainly, seeing pain contort his face.

"Yes, I can," he answered thoughtfully.

Colour darkened the man's face as he still wrestled with pain. The boy watched him steadily. His voice soft as breath he spoke to Peter.

"I forgive you; it's over, it's gone. I forgive you."

Peter looked up to him with struggling eyes, "But I did you wrong."

Joseph looked back steadily. "And I forgive the wrong so its gone."

The boy continued to chew slowly as his eyes lingered on the man. Seeing uncertainty cross his face he whispered, "And so does he."

Tears streamed from the man's face and glistened in the moonlight.

"How do you know?" Peter asked hesitantly.

"I think that's why he came." Joseph's voice grew strong as he remembered the King. "All of us are guilty of something; in some way we haven't done what we should have done, haven't been who we should have been. If we are honest, there are ways in which each one of us fails to be what the King wants us to be. In little ways or in big ways, we've all been like you, Peter, and run away from doing good in order to preserve ourselves, our own pleasure, safety or comfort." Joseph paused to look around at their faces crossed with discomfort. "And because we are all like this, all looking after ourselves instead of loving each other, the world ends up like this." He waved his arms towards the town. "Ugly. He died to buy us back."

The huddled forms looked at each other in the half-light. Their shadowed faces spoke of disbelief.

"Joseph, dear, you're tired; worn out by everything that has happened. Don't exhaust yourself thinking now." Her motherly voice soothed like honey.

"But the words say so, and I heard him speak, telling the whispering voice that he would buy us back with his own life." Joseph's voice stammered with desperate uncertainty. "Look at the words for yourself." He waved his arms despondently towards the dark walls.

Heads turned from side to side as they wondered what they were supposed to see.

"Look at what words?" they mumbled. "There's nothing here to see."

Joseph stumbled through the dark. "Come and look."

Mark shuffled hesitantly towards Joseph's voice and shadow.

"What am I looking for?" he asked.

"The walls are full of writing; all about him and his kingdom." Joseph's voice sang with excitement. "Look!" he squealed. "They're glowing again. Can you see?"

Mark peered carefully in silence. The others strained through the darkness to see and hear. Minutes passed.

"He's right!" Marks jubilant voice finally interrupted the heavy pause. "There are words here, hundreds of words carved over the walls. And they are the same stories; the ones my mother told me. They are true."

The others rushed over, exclaiming, "Where? Where?"

"Everywhere." Joseph spread his arms happily.

They poured over the words hungrily, with sighs and tears and murmurs of joy. Finally, with a voice distorted by emotion, Mark called their attention back.

"We mustn't forget why we have come out tonight. We must be quick or we'll miss our opportunity." The others concurred.

"What are we doing tonight?" Joseph enquired in a small voice.

The group fell silent until Mark spoke with a solemn note. "We are going to try to get his body down." He faltered as pain flooded his words. "To bury him properly," he blurted.

"But not you, Joseph. You can come home with me," the mother added quickly with reassuring kindness.

Joseph's mind was spinning as he felt his breath shortening. "No. I want to come too. Please. I want to help."

"You have seen enough, boy. You need to rest now." Mark's reply was short.

Joseph trembled with agitation, his thoughts whirling. He couldn't bear to be separated from his man.

"Where are you going to take him?" he asked tearfully.

The men looked at each other awkwardly. "We're not sure of the whole plan yet."

Joseph's words rushed out with his frantic thoughts. "I know a place. The perfect place. We can take him there tonight. I'll show you the way. I'll be fine. I'd rather be with you. I'll never sleep if you don't let me come."

The men looked at him and understood something of his pain and need to be involved. "O.K. We have to hurry. Soon the hooligans will be on the street and we'll be noticed."

Peering out of the great vaulted aperture of the Hall, into the dark, deserted square, the little group whispered to each other as their eyes scanned for movement. Hugging the shadows, the two men and boy slunk around the perimeter of the square under the cover of the empty buildings, making their anxious way towards the far end where the scaffolding still stretched upwards, etched across the white disc of the rising moon. The boy retched at the sight of the pale gleaming figure swinging slightly in the cool evening breeze. The figures froze as they heard footsteps snap along a nearby street. Their ears strained as they listened to their direction. Joseph's breath eased as he heard the footsteps turn away and grow faint. They began to edge forward again, noiselessly creeping towards the platform.

In a perilous moment, Mark's dark form darted forward. Leaping onto the stage, he lunged at the taut rope with a knife, sawing frantically at it until the man's body slumped forward into the waiting arms of the others. Smothering their groans of anguish and labour, they silently grasped the body and heaved it out of the square.

Squatting in the shadows of a wall, Mark whispered to Joseph, "We'll follow you then."

Deftly, Joseph wound through the lanes and backstreets in the quickest route he knew, to the only place he could take his man. The men gasped for breath as they struggled behind, their backs aching with the weight, sweat streaming. Finally, they forced their way through a broken portion of fence and found themselves huddling behind a small garden shed.

The men looked at the shed, doubt clouding their faces. "Are you sure?" they whispered.

"Absolutely," Joseph confirmed as he stepped up to the door. The door slid open noiselessly. Joseph peered cautiously in, straining to see anything in the thin moonlight. He beckoned for the others to follow. Mark swung the body over his shoulder and staggered in through the door, collapsing in the shelter of darkness inside. Peter crept in, pulling the door close behind him. The smell of damp earth filled their nostrils as they stood in the darkness, trying to silence their heaving breaths as they filled their aching lungs.

After a few panting minutes, Joseph began to feel his way blindly around the interior, running his hands over the surfaces, searching.

"What are you looking for, boy?" a voice whispered from the shadows.

"A candle and matches. There were some in here."

With a click, their startled faces were illuminated by a fading yellow beam of light. "I've got a torch." Peter's face was hidden in the darkness as Joseph looked blinking into the torchlight. "But the batteries are low, so better find those candles," he added. The small disc of light moved slowly around the space, climbing jerkily over rough wooden planks, dipping into corners, catching their anxious faces as they peered through the gloom. Suddenly the light halted as they all stared in shock and recoiled with repulsion.

"Is that a coffin?" Joseph's thin voice stammered fearfully, stating the obvious reality that they were all reeling over.

As the torchlight moved along the length of the shed, it revealed a coffin lying in the middle of the floor, its lid leaning against its side. Horrified, they all stared into its gaping interior.

"Is it a trap?" Mark's words were stretched with terror. "Were they expecting us?"

"Someone was expecting us. But who?"

Joseph's eyes searched for information as he struggled to control his distress. Next to the coffin were placed his father's hammer and a bag of nails. "Someone knew we would come here," he mused.

"Who knew about this place?" Mark interjected.

"He certainly did." Joseph slid his eyes towards the body that was lying by the wall. "But I don't know who else; or if we were ever followed here."

"I feel nervous. Maybe we are just standing in a trap? Can we lock the door." Peter's voice quivered with agitation.

"We can," Joseph replied thoughtfully, "if I can find the key. It used to always be above the door lintel." Stretching, he ran his fingers along the narrow ledge above the door. The sound of a metallic thud broke the uneasy silence. Joseph searched in the dull light for the fallen key. Grasping it, he turned it slowly in the rusty lock.

"What shall we do." he asked.

Eventually Mark spoke. "I think we should put him in the coffin and get out of here as fast as we can."

Everyone nodded in agreement, and together they grasped the body and heaved it into the open coffin. With grieving faces they slid the lid into place and solemnly tapped the nails deep into the wood. As sadness shook his boyish frame, Joseph drew his longing hand over the smooth, polished lid. His young fingers caressed the wood as his heart yearned for his king.

"We must go now. It's not safe." Peter tried gently to call Joseph away from the body, but his figure was bent over weeping. The men looked around awkwardly.

"Come on Joseph. Let's go home."

The boy slowly lifted his head and drew himself up. As his hands slid over the cover he felt the polished smoothness give way to roughness. Joseph ran his fingers along grooves that broke the surface; the wood was cut with an inscription.

"Bring the torch here," he beckoned urgently. "It feels like there is something carved into the wood."

Peter leaned over focusing the diminishing light on the wooden surface.

"You're right," he exclaimed in surprise.

They all peered intently at the inscription.

"What is it?" Peter screwed his face up in an effort to see.

Mark frowned. "It looks like a crown."

"It is a crown," Joseph exclaimed excitedly. "It's a crown."

"What does that mean? Peter asked shaking his head. "Why are you so pleased?"

Joseph sobbed with joy and emotion. "It means that it was Him who was expecting us. A crown is his symbol; the sign of a king. He knew we would bring him here and he prepared this."

The men wrestled with the information, trying to order their thoughts. Mark spoke cautiously.

"I still think we should be careful and get home now. We can come back tomorrow if it's safe and bury him properly." He stamped his foot on the thin wooden boards that formed the floor. "There should be earth under here. We can bury him here out of sight. But let's get home now and to bed."

"I'm staying here. This is my home. I don't want to leave him." Joseph spoke decisively, his eyes fixed on the ground.

The men sighed with fatigue. "You don't want to sleep with a dead body," they implored, too tired to argue with any vigour.

Joseph was resolved. "I will sleep in the bushes by the door."

"You'll freeze!"

"I have a sleeping bag!" he replied pointing to the mound of bedding piled in the corner.

The men shrugged wearily. "Do as you want. We'll be back tomorrow unless it looks like we are being followed."

Switching the torch off, Peter unlocked the door and opened it a crack, peering carefully outside. Beckoning with his head he moved stealthily into the shadows and disappeared.

Mark warned Joseph. "Keep out of sight and I'll see you tomorrow." He waited while the boy locked the door and crept into the bushes, then he was gone.

Joseph crawled into the warmth of the sleeping bag and looked up at the fragments of moon he could see glinting through the canopy of leaves and twigs that surrounded him. A faint breeze carried the night air, sweet with the smell of damp leaves and earth, across his face as his eyelids hung heavily and sleep crept like a fog over his weary mind.

His Name is Love

XII.

Hot sunshine slanted through the leafy branches as the sound of footsteps roused him from his stiff sleep. With sudden alarm, his eyes sprung open. He felt his heart pound as he lay frozen, listening. The steps moved again. Very slowly, so as to not make a sound, he strained to twist his head so he could see. Grass lawn spread out from his view, and the gravel path leading up to the shed. He waited, his breath held in apprehension.

Slow steps brought a pair of legs into sight; denim jeans and old trainers. Painfully, silently, he wriggled forward through the ground litter of leaves and twigs, to increase his view. The legs stopped in front of him. With suspended breath he waited, watching.

As Joseph looked up through the scratching branches and twigs, a face lowered itself to look down on him, meeting his gaze. Joseph's heart lurched with a paroxysm of hope and confusion. The face that was smiling down through the leaves was lined with familiarity and love. Joseph scrambled out of the bush to look at the figure properly. He stood up, squinting in the bright light, his mouth open in disbelief as he looked at the man's face. Trembling, he stretched his hand out to touch the man's arm, his fingers meeting warm flesh. He started in fear.

"Joseph, are you afraid of me." The voice was his too.

The startled boy ran to the shed, finding the door that he had locked flung wide open. He dug in his pocket, wrapping his fingers around the key that was still there. Anxiously, he stepped through the doorway and strained through the gloom to see the coffin. Its outline grew clear as his eyes adjusted to the half-light. He reeled as he saw that the lid was cast off and the wooden box was empty. His mind was spinning with the facts that were before him. He grasped the sides of the coffin and looked in, confirming the void. He turned the lid over with his hands; the crown inscription was still carved into the smooth wood.

The man was standing just outside the door. Joseph walked over to him.

"Is it really you?"

The man silently lifted his chin, opening the collar of his shirt. Around his neck Joseph could see the scorching marks of a rope. He untucked his shirt and pulled it up revealing a gaping but bloodless wound that had opened his chest.

Pallor blanched the boy's trembling face as he shrunk nauseously away.

"Are you a ghost?" he shuddered.

The man leant towards the recoiling boy, his face suffused with colour. He took Joseph's cold hands in his own, wrapping them in the warmth of his cupped hands. Bowing his head, he breathed a long, sweet breath of warm air over the boy's motionless fingers. Joseph cautiously lifted his eyes to meet the soft, shining gaze of the man.

"Do I seem like a ghost or a man?"

Joseph struggled to answer, his words stumbling in confusion. "You seem like a man, the same man; like him." His struggling words fell into an agonizing silence. "You seem to be him," he continued painfully, "but how can you be him. He was," he searched uncomfortably for words, "he is dead." His face fell despondently.

The man gently lifted the boy's hanging chin. "I was dead but now I'm not; I'm not a ghost but alive. I told you that I had a plan and this was all part of the plan." He examined the confusion and disbelief crossing Joseph's dark face. "If a person has created the order and matter of life with all its natural laws and governing principals, surely he himself must exist outside the limits and obligations of that world, ruling over it, interacting with it but not subject to it?"

Joseph stared dumbly in response.

"Think Joseph. Is it possible? Can it be that I, though assuming the form and appearance of someone from this world, actually exist outside this realm of reality; outside of time, nature, history and life as you know it? Think if this is possible. I know it is a strange concept to you, but is it possible?"

Joseph thought. There was no reason to assume that the limits of his knowledge defined the limits of reality. He had to concur that it was possible. He grunted a mumbled "Yes."

"What sort of king were you expecting?" the man continued.

Joseph questioned himself. His face reddened as he answered hesitantly. "Someone like my Dad only better; even wiser." He reflected for a minute. "Someone who could beat all the baddies and payback everyone who did evil."

The man chuckled affectionately. "That's a good answer in many ways. But I think you were still expecting someone like you; someone with your limitations even if he was quite good. You weren't expecting someone with power not only over good and evil, but over life and death itself." The man still saw doubt shadowing the boy's complexion. He looked Joseph directly in the eyes. "If I have existed eternally, without beginning and without end, and I made this world and life itself, do you think death in this world can really hold me? I allowed them to kill me so I could redeem you, buy you back from the one who has enslaved you all. But as Lord of life, I have risen; returned from the dead. Examine the evidence: I was dead, you know that; I am alive, you can see that. There is no trick; no deception."

Joseph considered the man's words. He spoke truly; he had been dead, now he was alive. And if these two realities are both true, he must have power over life and death, and be maker of all things. And if this is true, he must be King and Lord. And if he is Lord, Joseph's heart trembled not just in love but in awe, he must be worshipped and obeyed. Joseph felt his resistance melting as he allowed his mind to expand to encompass a truth that was more enormous and far reaching than any of his previous thoughts. In an instant he was filled with the overwhelming sense of his own minute proportion in the infinite and grand scale of reality that was opening up before his mind. He considered all his ambitions and independent notions in relation to the structure of reality that he was glimpsing; the impatient demands of temporal existence in the light of eternity. His small frame trembled as he bowed his head and sank reverently to his knees, clasping the man's feet in his hands and kissing them.

"I'm sorry," his small voice whispered, "I'm sorry that I haven't loved you as I should and I've disobeyed your laws, and tried to live for myself instead of serving you."

The boy felt firm hands pass over his head, smoothing

his dishevelled hair; and grasp him gently around his shoulders, raising him up to his feet. The man's radiant eyes searched Joseph deeply.

"I forgive you."

Joseph's mind still struggled. "If you exist in this other dimension, why did you bother with me and my life?"

The man smiled as he answered. "Because I love you. This makes your life immeasurably significant; love. And because of this love," he continued, "I came to restore things; to make a way for everyone to come back to me; to know my love."

"But it doesn't look like anything has been restored. It looks worse than ever," the boy questioned painfully.

The man's gaze shifted to a distant place. "Don't look just at the appearance of things. Evil has been defeated with a final certainty that makes beings you don't see or even know about shudder. He will play out his last moves, ever denying the reality that he will also have to face, and he will cause pain and suffering, but he will have no victory. The real battle has already been fought."

The man's eyes returned to Joseph. "I'm only here for a while. Listen carefully. I must return to my Kingdom shortly but I will come back for you soon. Wait for me and don't lose faith. You must remember the things you have seen and do not give in to doubt. But first I must show myself to the others; otherwise they will never believe you," he added knowingly.

"They will be at the house of the mother. We can take a secret route." The boy's voice was drumming with excitement.

"I know exactly where they are, but today we will take the open route. Nothing is to be hidden anymore.

It's time for you to be my witness, to tell people who I am."

The man, bold, and the boy, squirming, walked along the road, under the intense and malicious scrutiny of the shocked onlookers. Newspapers rustled in outrage as their pages were flung open to identify the criminal pictured inside, "confirmed dead". Muttering words pursued him as he called to them with his smiling eyes.

"I saw him hanging with my own eyes," bewildered voices mouthed.

Joseph pushed along the road, trying to escape the glaring and disbelieving eyes. He darted into the doorway of the woman's house, flapping at the man to follow quickly. He rapped impatiently at the closed door, shuffling from foot to foot with apprehension. As the door edged open he rushed in, pushing the surprised woman back in his haste. As she staggered to regain her balance she glanced furtively at the people gathering in the street; a sparse crowd of people trailing indecisively with gaping, inquisitive faces.

Perplexed and frightened, she shrunk into the dark protection of the hall, squeezing the door close. As the occluding door almost eclipsed her retreating face, she suddenly froze, arrested by a face that called out to her in recognition. Warmth flooded through her skin as her eyes scanned hopefully, resting in amazement on his face, as he took slow steps towards her.

"Can you believe it is me?" he called to her, smiling.

She nodded with trembling mouth and glistening eyes that clung to him as he drew closer. Her voice rang out in a sobbing call, as she pulled the door open. "Come and see who is here. Come and welcome your King."

XIII.

The boy tossed in his troubled sleep; dreams still disturbed him as he whimpered softly in the night and tried to hold onto his father. He wrestled his eyes open to escape the perpetual flames and tearing heart. The moonlight crept as a narrow band of silver, through the gap between the curtains. His eyes flitted around the dim room, grasping familiar objects to draw him out of his past. He turned to the twin bed pushed neatly against the wall, and searched for the curve of his stretching form, rising and falling with each peaceful breath.

He stared harder as the man's shape remained hidden in the shadow. Perplexed, he sat up and rubbed his eyes. Letting his feet drop silently onto the cold floor, he padded over with searching, outstretched arms. His fingers bumped against the soft mattress, and felt for the crumpled covers and sleeping form of his friend. As his hands slid forward over the crisp, taught bed with its neat tucks and smooth, turned sheet, he knew that the King had left.

Shivering, he crawled back into bed and hugged his blankets. He had been anticipating this moment each day that the King had spent with them; precious days of sitting together around the table, listening to him as he had explained everything to them concerning himself and his Kingdom; days when his heart had expanded with joy as he had drunk in every light-filled detail. Now, he lay in bed feeling his own chest rise and fall, and waited for the terrible absence to envelope him with crushing finality; a relentless wave of desolation. He felt the purple hues of sadness seep gently into the edges of his heart with pricking pangs and subside. As he lay, motionless, in the inky contours of the night, he felt something solid and reassuring grow in the depths of his being; a warm sense of certainty enlarge within him, strengthening his fragile mind, pushing back the gloom. The boy's eyelids rested softly on his downy cheeks and he slept.

XIV

The fresh winds swept dust and litter as a stinging shower into the face of Joseph as he perched on the scaling white stone steps, surrounded by an untidy ring of people sprawled around him; faces trained intently on the boy's moving lips as he answered their questions, and laboured carefully to explain all that he had learnt.

"But what does it have to do with life now? It just seems irrelevant to me." The voice was hard and accusing.

Joseph exhaled slowly as he allowed his thoughts to organise and his exasperation to settle. Speaking slowly he repeated the essence of what he had been working to communicate for some time.

"All most people can see is this day to day life that surrounds us, and they strive to make it worthwhile; to be happy, comfortable, fulfilled. They live as if there is nothing more. But what we see now is a tiny part of our whole life. Life doesn't end when we die, it just continues somewhere else. This life here will end quite quickly, what ever we make of it. We should put more thought into our lives that will go on forever. If you don't chose to love him and live with him now, you will have to live without him forever."

"But that doesn't bother me," the voice retorted. "I haven't missed him so far."

"Just now you live in a world full of his goodness and love, like a light that shines on everything making it better. Imagine the world if you took all goodness, kindness and love out of it. That's what life without him will be like. When he's gone you will suddenly realise that he was here but you didn't recognise him.

He made us to love him and be loved by him," Joseph implored, "to be a picture of his love and beauty. We can't do that if we don't even want to know who he is." The boy rested, weary from concentration.

"So, basically, your life makes sense to you because you believe there is an afterlife and the purpose of this life is earning your way there," another voice chimed in imperiously. "No harm in that if it makes you feel your life is worthwhile, as long as you don't go around annoying people by suggesting that we need to join in your little delusion." He snickered triumphantly to the faces around him.

"We don't earn our way there," Joseph explained, suppressing his annoyance. "You don't understand. We can never do anything good enough to deserve being with him. Each one of us has turned our back on him, and started to love ourselves and our lives more than him; even though he loves us we have chosen to live without him, by our own rules instead of his."

Joseph's eyes roamed over the faces strewn around him, then searched the blue expanse of sky as he laboured to find an adequate way of expressing this truth.

"We are like children who have taken all the good things our parents have given us, and gone off to enjoy them without loving or even thanking our parents in return. Wouldn't you be upset if the child you loved left you and denied your existence? He wants us back because he loves us and wants to forgive us, not because we are so good we deserve to be accepted. Without knowing it, we have joined sides with his enemy, believing his lies and following his ways. The enemy has made you his slave; he lures you by promising you everything you want most, but he will lead you into a very lonely place and leave you there with nothing. But the King loves you and wants you to be part of his family. He has bought us back with his own life. But if you want to be with him you have to love him; you have to admit that you need rescuing and trust him to save you."

"But I don't need rescuing," a voice spluttered in indignation. "I've spent my whole life trying to be good, being kind and helpful to others. What is your King like if this is not good enough? Pretty picky."

"He's perfect, that's what he's like. But he knows you can't be perfect. He wants you to admit it so that he can forgive you and change you to be like him." The boy stood up and looked around the gathered crowd. "We always measure our own goodness by the standards we see around us, which are pretty low, rather than by comparing ourselves to what we should be like. We should be like Him. We think we are a lot better than we actually are."

"If he knows we can't be perfect, why does he judge us for it?" a cross voice called across to him.

"He can judge fairly because only he actually sees things as they really are; he sees and knows everything; he doesn't just see our actions but he knows our thoughts and motives as well. If he is the all powerful creator and he does not deal with evil, but just turns a blind eye and doesn't call anyone to account, then he would be just as bad. To tolerate evil is evil," the boy carefully reasoned.

"So why doesn't he deal with the really bad people and leave the rest of us alone," someone puzzled.

"Where would you draw the line with evil?" Joseph threw the question back. "What level of evil is O.K. and what's too bad? I guess we'd always draw the line beneath our self. He judges everyone the same, but gives everyone a chance to be forgiven. That's fair, isn't it?"

An indignant voice cut in from the edge of the crowd. "I resent the fact that you presume to judge the quality or value of my life; I can live a satisfying life without reference to any myths of future life or a King. My life has value because I inject it with meaning as I live."

Joseph lowered his eyes with a sinking sense of defeat. "I'm not making a judgement about your life; I'm sure it is more pleasant than mine. But we cannot live without reference to the King. He exists and every aspect of life has reference to him."

"That is what you believe," she retorted.

"That is the reality that exists, believe it or not," Joseph replied wearily.

"How do you know he exists?" another voice taunted.

Joseph's eyes brightened and his words rang with confidence. "Because for a brief time he lived in our town, walked out streets, and did things that no ordinary man can do. He looked like a man but he was beyond an ordinary man. Just look at the evidence and judge for yourself."

The disgruntled speakers fell away from the crowd and mingled back into the darting streams of people that criss-crossed the square.

A soft voice in gentle, enquiring tones reached out to Joseph. "Can you tell me what he's like?"

Joseph's heart lifted as his words, gilded with light, flowed out into the hearts of the hearers, filling them with the same joy. Their minds reeled with pictures of the splendours of his kingdom, the riches of his love, the depths of his compassion and dimensions of his goodness.

"I want to know this King and live with him." A small voice piped with child-like simplicity into the murmuring reflections. "How can I?"

Warmth swelled in Joseph's heart at the sound of this simple enquiry. "Believe him; Believe that he is the King of everything, and that he has paid the full price to bring you back into his Kingdom; be sorry that you have hurt him with your disobedience and lack of love; love him and honour him with your life and he will forgive you and give you everlasting life."

A sudden shout and scuffle broke the gentle speech. A dull thud cracked the back of Joseph's head pounding him forward onto the ground where his face smacked into the hard, stinging stone. Pain and nausea shot through his head as he weakly lifted himself up on his arms. Blood drizzled from his grazed face and his swelling lips throbbed painfully. He blinked to bring the swimming crowd into focus as he looked timidly around for the cause of his assault. Cowering, he looked dizzily up at the heavy booted men that had stepped into his view. Around him the people were jumping to their feet and staggering away with wails and moans. Sparse voices raised themselves up against the abuse, hotly calling for justice, but fierce growls silenced and scattered them. Trembling, he waited for the next blow. A red face pushed itself rudely towards him, bloated with anger, purple lips contorted to expose yellowing teeth. Saliva spurted with his brutal words.

"The King does not exist and it is an offence to say he does." The man's eyes were bulging with fury.

"It's against the law to speak about a King who does not exist! Why do you fear him if he doesn't exist?" Joseph's words earned him a savage kick in the side. The winded boy groaned silently as he gripped his screaming flesh.

"Pick him up," the voice grunted coarsely, "and bring him to the gallows."

Joseph's feet stumbled down the stairs as he was picked up and dragged briskly by two thick arms. Head reeling with sickness, he staggered and sank between the two heavy set men who grasped him, one at each side. Nauseously, he saw the cobbled square rush under him as pain gripped his wrenched arms. Around him people scattered like flighty pigeons, and as he lifted his swooning head he could see the gallows approaching like a charging assault. As they reached the sombre shadows stretching from the timber scaffolding, the pace slowed, then halted. Joseph raised his hanging head to see that a small party had already assembled.

As Joseph was shoved onto his feet, an imperious voice spoke to those present.

"Found guilty of the charges of treason and disturbing the peace, he is sentenced to death by hanging. The prisoner will be brought..." His officious voice was cut suddenly short by an angry scream.

"No!"

All heads swung around in surprise to see a woman running towards them frantically.

"Stop. What are you doing?" she demanded, fear rising in her voice.

The men turned their faces away from her. A dark whisper rose from among them and hissed viciously, "Do it quickly."

"You can't execute him without a proper trial," she pressed urgently. "What has happened to law and order in this town?"

Desperately, Joseph searched the men's faces as they communicated silently with the exchange of looks and subtle movements of the brow. An older man with spectacled eyes blinking blindly turned to her, and smiling grimly with thin, tight lips, spoke in a steel voice.

"Madam, I am law and order," he snarled. "Step aside so justice can be carried out." He pushed the trembling mother aside with a swipe of his heavy arm.

Quivering with agitation she pulled at his suited sleeve desperately. The mayor brushed her aside with annoyance and turned back to the pale, stricken figure of Joseph.

Joseph shrunk fearfully as he saw the grim, shadowy form swelling and enveloping the group of men, breathing evil resolution into their hard minds. As the woman implored and wailed desperately, the Mayor coughed, politely covering his mouth with a thin, pale hand, and glancing down at his papers, he continued. to speak in a smug monotone.

"The prisoner will be escorted to the place of execution for immediate carrying out of the sentence."

The stone-faced men stared superiorly as Joseph was grasped rudely and dragged, tripping, up the rough wooden steps, deaf to the hysterical sobs and wails of the mother.

Joseph was numb with shock as he found himself lifted above the heads of gathering people, swaying nauseously on the creaking timber boards, as gripping hands led him with hard shoves. His mind was washed with apprehension and rushing dread as he felt the coarse, pricking rope pass over his head and press like a tight band around his throat. He felt fear spread through his body in sharp, pulsating waves, disconnecting his reason, spilling over in trembling sobs. Every fibre of his flesh quivered uncontrollably as his roving eyes passed unseeing over the pale upturned faces before him.

In a breaking moment of gleaming light, Joseph's mind soared upwards with silver clarity. Into his mind rushed the dazzling reality of all his hopes. "If I die I will be with him always. That is what I long for." With all the power of his mind he held onto that shining, light-filled thought. Fear drained away as gentle waves of joy crept through him, easing his trembling limbs and strengthening his heart. Weakly, he turned the corners of his mouth into a smile which he directed towards the tear-stained face of the mother.

Lightening split the sky with an echoing crack which whipped and thundered. Every figure was dashed to the ground in crushing fear. Gasping faces, stricken with terror, searched desperately above as they cowered helplessly. Silence followed with paralysing power. They all waited, motionless.

Fire burst into the heavens and blazoned with roaring ferocity, searing the sun. Everyone moaned with anguish as they crawled like scattering ants, desperate for cover.

Joseph stood stiffly on the wooden platform, neck still gripped by the rough rope, watching the white faces,

distorted with fear, mill around in wild confusion. More
flames shot through the skies, bathing them in crimson
light. As the people staggered chaotically around,
Joseph observed the lurking, shadowy figure circle and
enclose the Mayor and his men. They bent their heads
together in an anxious, muttering conference, cringing
fearfully at the explosions of light. They shuffled in a
dark mass, inching their terrified way towards Joseph
who stared at them disbelievingly.

The ground rocked and shuddered in a violent,
wrenching movement that flung them, wailing, to the
ground. Joseph felt the rope pull painfully against his
throat as he struggled to keep himself upright. Bricks
and masonry showered and slid to the ground as great
cracks splintered the creaking buildings. Everyone
clung fearfully to any solid thing within reach; others
were splayed on the cobbled ground as it bucked and
shook. Finally, the shaking eased and stopped, and
stillness returned with a strange unease.

The Mayor was quick to get to his feet, brushing dust
from his dark suit as he continued determinedly up the
stairs with a grim expression. Joseph, who's chaffed
neck was searing with pain, felt cold rush through his
body as he saw the Mayor and his black mentor
approach him hurriedly, mumbling viciously. Joseph
glanced around at the confusion and mayhem; the
square littered with bodies strewn and cowering, debris
flung across the cobbles, a cloud of dust casting a haze
over the scene of ruin. His relief at feeling the ground
become solid and still, evaporated as he felt the dark
figure rush at him venomously.

Their progress was halted suddenly by a low rumble
which rolled across the earth and spread through every

stone and timber, echoing from building to building. Quivering with apprehension, the Mayor grasped the rope knotted around Joseph's slim neck and tightened it. Joseph spluttered as he sucked air noisily.

Small stones danced as the ground trembled and the distant noise of thunder grew louder. Every face turned fearfully towards the far end of the square as the rumble grew into a crashing percussion; a rhythmic beating of ringing hooves thundering like a storm. Sparks of lightening glittered and streaked in rainbow hues, dazzling like jewels.

The Mayor froze, his face ashen, his limp mouth gaping in horror. Joseph's eyes searched uncomprehending but he felt joyous anticipation growing uncontrollably in his bursting heart. As the thundering noise almost broke tumultuously over the waiting crowd, its tempo suddenly changed into a stately march; the ringing hooves falling in a precise beat of dignity and poise. The gasping crowd retreated like a receding tide; shrinking into a dense mass at the foot of the gallows as the snorting breath of horses could be heard over their ringing hooves.

Joseph saw the billowing flag first; a great banner of red silk, writhing and unrolling in the breeze; its gold trim dancing in the sun. Blazoned across the centre in pure gold was the insignia of a crown. Joseph felt his chest swell with happiness and his voice leap forward in praise. He saw the legs of a white horse stretch and strike the ground as they moved lightly in a graceful trot. His eyes rushed over the smooth curve of the horse's neck, as it turned beautifully, gliding like a swan, into the square, and skirted longingly up to the face of the rider. He drew his breath sharply. Astride the horse was a figure so magnificent that every eye was fixed on him as he approached majestically.

For a moment Joseph's heart skipped unevenly. The face was familiar but different; illumined with a strange light, it almost shone; the deep eyes seemed to flicker with fire. His head glittered with a crown and he was dressed in the finest robes of gold and indigo. From his powerful hand stretched a glinting sword which flashed beams of light as the rider drove it forward towards the screaming, retreating crowd of people. Behind him, rows and rows of white horses followed in sweeping waves; astride them, hundreds of figures dressed in flowing robes of brilliant white. Precise in step and formation, they advanced into the square in formal strides, filling and surrounding it with impenetrable, gleaming white.

All the horses came to a standstill; eyes fixed ahead, drumming hooves silent. The crowd looked back in wonder. With a shuffle of feet and clanking of bridle, the King's horse took a step forward; then in slow steps paced regally towards the gallows. As he approached, the light of his eyes fell across the upturned faces, and in one voice, a sigh issued from their trembling lips and spread through the crowd. Like a falling wave, men and women fell, sobbing, to their knees. For a few, their faces were wet with tears that spilled over from the joy exploding in their hearts as they feasted on the object of their love and hope. But, for most, their tears were agonised streams bleeding from hearts wracked with remorse.

The Mayor froze in his guilty pose, staring horrified ahead. He heard the black voice spitting commands at him, raging against his inactivity.

"Kill the boy. Do it now," the dark voice snarled.

The Mayor struggled to obey but the flame-filled eyes bore into him, and he found his knees bending against his will as he bowed down and joined in the chorus that was echoing around the square, "Hail the King!"

The dark figure rushed towards Joseph, seething with frustration, swollen with hate, and grasped the boy's neck in his strangling hands.

"Stop," the King thundered. "Leave him alone."

The dark being shuddered and answered in a thin, rasping voice, "He's mine. I can do what I like with him."

"He's not." The King's voice penetrated like his gleaming sword, cutting truth from lies. "You know he is mine. I paid the full price and he's mine."

The dark being quivered and squirmed, his heart growing blacker and fouler in desperation.

"What price did you pay?" he stammered weakly, his rebellious eyes sinking away from the piercing gaze.

Eyes flicked up questioningly from bowing heads as they awaited his reply. The silence continued. In a slow deliberate movement, the King rose in his stirrups until he was standing above the heads of all the other horsemen, and began to loosen the fastenings of the great gilded cloak that hung from his shoulders and wrapped around him. The cloak slipped away from his heaving shoulders, revealing the white of his linen tunic. The crowd gasped in unison as they saw it was soaked and streaked with deep crimson blood.

"The price I paid is my life," was the King's certain reply. "And anyone who believed in me, who knew me as their King, is free to come with me. The rest are yours."

His eyes burned at the cringing dark figure who was already slipping away at the sound of the King's voice. He turned around to the bowing mass of people.

"You all made a choice and now you will have to live by it." His voice faltered with sadness. "I wanted you to all be with me, but so many of you refused. Instead, you chose him." His eyes flashed at the disappearing shadow. "I wanted to love you and give you life, but all he wants is to enslave you and puff himself up on your praise."

He lowered himself into the saddle and urged the horse forward. People scattered as he rode through them and up to the raised wooden platform. He leapt onto the boards and placing a gentle hand on Joseph's head, he sliced through the rope with his gleaming sword. Grasping the boy around the waist, he swung himself back onto his horse, sitting Joseph across the withers. He swung the horse around with a flick of the reins and called out a command to the multitude of riders.

"Take all who are ours and leave the rest."

There was a shuffle of hooves as horses stepped out of the ranks and rode off, some into the waiting crowd, others into distant parts of the town. Joseph watched with amazement as riders located particular people and swung them powerfully onto their own horses; people who with shining faces were waiting to be found. Joseph looked with distress at the faces remaining.

"Can we not take them? It seems so awful to leave them behind."

"They wouldn't come if you tried to bring them. They prefer the darkness to the light. Look ahead, Joseph, not behind." The King's voice was deep with sorrow.

The silvery horses all returned to their position. The King gave a shout and his horse leapt into a canter, bounding lightly across the square with the rows of riders following in close waves. The ground thundered and the buildings rattled as they swept away; a foaming sea of white horses shrinking from sight. And as the last flicking tail of white swished out of sight, twilight descended over the square with an impenetrable gloom and desolation, as the cold shadows enlarged and enveloped each groaning heart.

XV.

The wind rushes cold in Joseph's face, pricking tears from his smarting eyes. He smiles at the King who holds him close with strong, encircling arms. The King's eyes are bright again as they bound away from the darkness, galloping towards the shining city, the palace of gold that shimmers ahead of them. Grass rushes under the beating hooves that press faster and faster. They are soaring smoothly as rocks and trees are swept away, shrinking beneath them as they rise higher and higher. The golden palace is growing before them, gliding closer as they speed ahead; hooves beating the air. A silver ribbon winds through the mountains, a glittering trail leading to the wide city gates. The horses sweep down in graceful curves, feet touching down in front of the gates. The King swings silently to the ground, placing Joseph carefully beside him. He nods to the waiting riders who do the same. With a whisper the horses turn and gallop off into the rolling pastures tossing their snowy manes.

Excitement builds as they walk together, following the singing river as it splashes brightly. Joseph's eyes are wide with anticipation, his legs skipping eagerly. The King stops at the bank of the rushing river and beckons him forward; inviting, calling.

"This is where you must cross," the King insists, waving his arm towards the plunging waters.

Joseph grins and steps forward hesitantly. Casting a quick look around him, he springs trustingly away from the bank.

His breath is snatched from him as he smacks against the hard, cold water and is rolled dizzily, nauseously in its depths. Darkness surrounds him as he tumbles helplessly, his arms and legs flailing uselessly against the overpowering currents. His chest heaves as he struggles against the pounding, suffocating water, his limbs grasping desperately for air.

"Help," he wails in a smothered cry.

Firm hands grasp his sides and lift his head above the churning rush of water. Joseph gasps and splutters, drawing in air thirstily. Terrified, he grips the arms that encircle him, as his legs still thrash in the current. The sound of a deep voice drives away his clutching fear.

"I've got you. Don't struggle. I've been at your side the whole time. You couldn't have drowned."

Tears burst from the boy's eyes as he wrestles with his fear.

"Listen to me. I want you to put your feet on the ground and hold my hand, and we'll walk through this river together." The King's voice is calm and persuading.

The boy straightens his knees and stretches his toes hesitantly down, unconvinced. Unexpectedly, his foot strikes against the sandy bottom of the river bed. With the currents still rushing against his small body, he places his feet on the bottom and stands.

"Good," the King smiles. "Now let go of my arms and take my hand."

The boy cautiously loosens his grip on the man's arm and slides his hand into the man's waiting palm.

"Now walk," the King urges him.

While the water still rages dangerously around his chin and buffets his thin legs, Joseph makes his steady way towards the far bank with the King beside him. Gradually his head rises higher and higher above the splashing water, until his shoulders are free, then his chest and abdomen. Eventually the water is washing playfully at his knees and shins as he strides through the sparkling waves. His hand is still nestled deep within the King's enfolding grip.

As Joseph's feet swing clear of river and stamp on the solid earth of the bank, he looks thankfully up at the King. A muffled squeal of surprised erupts in his throat. Puzzled, he stares at the King.

"You are smaller," he murmurs, confused.

"No, Joseph," the King laughs, "you are bigger. You aren't a boy any more, You've grown up into a man."

Joseph runs his bewildered eyes down the length of his altered body. He gasps to find that his dirty, worn trousers have vanished and he is no longer wearing his old, frayed shirt. His boyish frame has stretched and broadened into that of a man and is robed in dazzling white linen, cut like the clothes of a prince. As he glances back across the river he sees streams of people emerging from its icy waters, gleaming like new creatures in their clothes of glistening white. Their faces are young and fresh, smoothed free of guilt and anxiety, their step is light and full of joy. They are a surging multitude pouring out of the river and through the open gates, waved forward by the beckoning arms of the King who welcomes them joyfully into his palace.

Joseph's feet skip as he dances towards the massive doors ahead of him. Light floods over him as he passes through the doorway, gaping at the huge room which opens up in its cavernous proportions. His eyes skip over all the wondrous detail, of luminous gold and light leaping like crystal from precious gems, and skirt hungrily across to the stretching table, mounded high with plates of food, and lined with the expectant faces of seated figures. From down the length of the long room he can hear murmurs of joy erupting and bubbling happily. The stream of white robed people flow into the room and swell around him like a sea of searching, sparkling faces. Eyes jump from one waiting face to another, until with a short breath of delight they are found, and rush to occupy one of the vacant seats.

The King touches Joseph on the shoulder and points with an outstretched arm. Joseph's eyes follow his direction. A group of faces are waving excitedly to him. Joseph peers ahead.

"Go on Joseph," the King urges affectionately. Joseph walks uncertainly towards the waving group of people. As he gets closer he runs with sudden recognition, and rushes laughing towards them. The King smiles as he watches the family reunite with embraces and kisses.

Like a foamy wave that rushes and breaks over the thirsty sand, sinking and disappearing into the grainy shore before it can retreat, so the gleaming stream of white figures washes into the room and is absorbed into the rows of waiting people, so that the table swells with shining faces. Joseph scans the table brimming with waiting people; only the place directly opposite him is still empty.

The King stands, watching as each person finds their place. The babble of chatter and laughter slides away into a swirling note that rises in a tune as every voice joins in one rejoicing song. The King's eyes glide over each of the jubilant faces lining the long table; sweeping down one side, running up the other, then turning slowly to the one figure still standing, observing.

His Name is Love

She stands silently, back pressed to the wall, watching with an aching heart, invisible to all but the King; unnoticed but silently observing. She feels His eyes rest on her and her breath quickens, her heart beats with sharp pain. She turns her eyes shyly towards the brilliant light, blinking cautiously, filled with dread and joy.

His voice whispers like a thundering waterfall. "It's time for you to go. Remember what you have seen and make your choice."

She keeps her eyes fastened to the radiant light of his face as all else fades and darkness creeps across like a veil, obscuring the singing faces. She struggles as the vast chamber shrinks and disappears, clutching the glowing embers of silver light in her heart as her sight fails and darkness blankets her.

His Name is Love

XVI.

With a jolt she gasps and convulses violently. Electric pain sears her chest and courses rudely through her fragile body. The scorching light draws near, drilling through the darkness, searching the dark recesses of her mind. Distant voices call urgently, hammering words growing louder. Noise bursts painfully into her mind; a din of jarring sounds that clank and beep in alarm, footsteps squeaking on vinyl floors, a blur of sounds jabbing intrusively, and somewhere a low wail sounding relentlessly like a horn. She coughs and shudders, retching against the gagging pain in her throat, the pressure of air squeezing against her frail breath. The voices rise in flapping intensity as she struggles weakly to pull against the burning pain in her throat, her arms thrashing helplessly. Sharp pain jabs her flesh as she pulls and bends against the tubes and cannulas of stiff plastic and piercing metal. Her arms are pressed heavily to her side as she writhes in confusion; the round light glaring through the fog.

"Miriam, Miriam." Her dulled mind slowly recognises her name calling in the grey haze.

"It's me," she screams loudly in the thinning clouds of her mind, but her lips stumble and slur, mumbling an incoherent groan.

The snapping orders slide into distinction as she forces her mind to swim through the confusion; layers of voices rising over each other, and beneath a deep murmuring stream, pressing, reassuring. The wailing stops and relief spreads immediately. Shadows break the painful glare of the burning light as bustling people lean over her.

"Miriam, if you can hear me open your eyes."

She labours with her sealed lids, struggling vainly. In a flashing second, a glimpse of bleached white, of starched blue linen and peering faces leaps into her mind, then the darkness slams over her eyes and she tumbles nauseously. The voices around her jump in excitement.

"She did it. She heard. Did you see that Mrs. Lowe? She opened her eyes."

She sinks exhausted and slides into the darkness, feeling the voices hover around her, the hands press, her throat burns. A sharp anxiety stirs in her breast. "There is something I must remember." She tries to hold her drifting mind as the sounds mumble and stray. "Help me remember," she pleads vaguely as her thoughts fragment.

A clear, brilliant light, soothing not glaring, grows steadily before her, whispering love in murmuring tones, driving away her fear.

"I remember. I choose you," she sighs and drifts into sleep.

When she wakens the room is still except for the gentle motion of a hand stroking her hair. Machines softly pump and whir, a gentle sighing breath whispers at her side. Her eyes float around the low-lit room. She slowly turns her head towards the breath that warms her cheek. She gazes into her mother's large, frightened eyes, shiny with tears.

"Mamma!" Her voice is hoarse. She swallows painfully.

Her mother presses her quivering lips to her daughter's pale forehead. "Don't speak now, rest," she whispers.

"I must speak," she struggles, "I must tell you what I've seen."

"What have you seen?" her mother asks sweetly.

"There is a palace with a wonderful King living in it. He is like shining light, like a rainbow, like all the precious jewels of the whole world shining together." She hesitates. All her words seem dull and lifeless, failing to give any taste of the reality she had witnessed.

"He is sort of stern and very, very kind at the same time," she continues hesitantly. "He can see inside you and know what you are thinking. Anyway, he killed the evil one who was making the world bad, and took everyone who loved him to live in his palace for ever." She falls silent and looks at her mother sadly. "I love you so much Mamma, and Daddy. I don't want to make you sad. But I can't stay here very long. I want to go back to Him."

"To who darling?" her mother enquired gently.

" To Him; the King. To live in his palace with him."

"But darling, he's not real. He's just a dream you've had." Her mother soothes her head again with her long fingers which twirl strands of her lifeless hair."

Tears burst into her eyes. "But he is real and you must believe that he is real because only people that believe he is real and love him can live with him, and I want you to come and live with Him too. Please believe Mamma. You will like him so much."

Anxiety pricks at the mother's heart but she steadies her voice. "How can I believe in him if I don't know who he is?"

The little girl smiles in happiness. "If you want to know Him, I shall tell you all about Him." And with her small girlish voice she takes her mother back into the sparkling palace and reveals every wonderful thing.

A garden suffused with early morning sunshine floats like perfume through her dry, boring pain; a fleeting glimpse of his face glows in her thoughts as she drifts in her nausea. A smile flickers briefly across her chalky face as she struggles with a feeble attempt to lift her head off the stiff pillow.

"You're here early today, Mama. Lovely," she sighs, as she gives up trying to lift herself and sinks back into the pillow. Anguish creases her wan face as she examines her mother's raw eyes and blotchy complexion. "You've been crying again."

Her mother sniffs and stretches her lips into a smile. "It's nice to see you," she remarks slowly, trying to avoid the awful reality.

"Come closer," the girl whispers beckoning with her thin hand.

Her mother is confused by her daughter's strange happiness but perches awkwardly on the edge of her bed.

"I know I am dying." She lies breathless from words and emotion, but her eyes show a determination to continue. "You're all afraid to tell me but I know. I'm not afraid, mamma. He's there so don't be afraid for me."

Pain flashes across her mother's face.

"You don't believe, but I've found a book all about Him. Look in the cupboard," she pants exhausted.

Her mother swivels to face the small hospital closet abutting her bed, tears welling again in her eyes.

"What book darling?" she asks as she rummages through the small clutter of possessions.

"That red one," the girl indicates.

The mother examines it suspiciously in silence, eventually turning to speak. "But it's a bible, dear. It's not real either."

"Read the pages I've marked."

The mother flicks through the book, fearfully turning the pages. Her eyes scan the print, rolling over the lines of words, scooping up sentences from the marked pages, mumbling distractedly; "His eyes were like flames of fire, His voice was like the roar of waters; had the appearance of jasper and carnelian; around the throne was a rainbow; seated on a white horse; called faithful and true; clothed in a robe dipped in blood; He has the name written, 'King of kings and Lord of lords'"

"Read the next bit to me please," she asks

"Behold," the mother coughs and struggles with her trembling voice, "the dwelling place of God is with man. He will dwell with them and they will be his people, and God himself will be with them as their God. He will wipe away every tear from their eyes, and death shall be no more, neither shall there be mourning nor crying nor pain anymore, for the former things have passed away."

"It's nice," the girl sighs.

The mother agrees with nodding head, her eyes still held by the page.

"Hold my hand, Mama," she whispers in a distant, strangled voice. The white planes of the walls dissolve into a shifting haze that closes over her, pressing close, pushing back the muffled sounds of hospital. Only her mother's warm face appears through the fog, leaning above, her eyes round pools of blue, her mouth sounding silent words as anguish fills her fading face. Her mother's face is wrenched in a scream that is lost in the humming silence that carries the girl away. The lilting tunes of singers fills her mind as wisps of fog blur her mother's face. The cloudless blue of the azure sky slips into her heart drenching her in light; she floats on the cusp of joy. She shouts back from the humming tunes and exploding light, "He is real." Her lips move around silent words and her mother's face moves further and further away, disappears into the shrouding wisps of white. But the moment her mother slips out of sight, the mist vanishes and she gazes into His face; suffused with all the light of the sun, smiling with all the love of heaven, a crown circling his head.

Her voice joins in the ringing love song that circles His kingdom, floating through the warm garden, and filling the endless sky. He takes her hand and leads her across the rolling lawns of green, daubed with spring colour, through the glades of trees, towards the splashing stream. He drops her hand, and stooping, cups his hands in the cool water, drawing the sparkling liquid up to her waiting lips.

"Drink," he tells her. As her lips part he pours the living water into her mouth. "And I will give you water to drink that will well up to a spring of eternal life."

He leads her to the gnarled, ancient tree hung with life-drenched fruit. He stretches up, reaching for a piece of fruit which falls easily into his hand. He offers it up to her, saying, "Now may you eat of the tree of life." Grasping it in her hands, she draws it to her mouth and bites, her eyes never leaving his as she swallows the fruit.

The juice still sweet on her lips he leads her further into the shining garden, laughing with all the swaying stems heaped with flowers, all the bounding animals, all the bowing trees. The garden slips away as they skip over ascending mountains, running beside the dazzling stream. The golden palace grows nearer, light arching off its glittering walls, voices ringing in a resplendent chord.

Her dancing feet step lightly as she follows the surging river, drawn gently forward by his leading hand. Her eyes rush ahead in anticipation as she passes over every familiar sight. The great door arches overhead, welcoming her inside. She steps forward with thrills of expectation, her heart pounding with longing.

Her feet stop at the foot of the long table and her eyes sweep along the extent of the stretching room. She finds herself in the same instance as when she left, as if time had not moved from when she had stood watching the room fill with shining people. The King's hand presses gently against her back, urging her forward. She sees a young man rise from his chair and bow courteously to her. With a wave of his hand he beckons her into the vacant seat opposite. His warm face draws her silently to her place and she slips into the waiting seat.

The singing voices shimmer like sunlight glancing off clear pools of water. His voice is a fountain of music and light cascading above.

"Please eat."